"Kalani Bishop, w  **honor of being my**

He pressed his lips toget
he finally nodded. "I gue

"Yay!" Lana leaped into his arms and hugged him close. She buried her nose in his neck, drawing in his cologne. The familiar scent of her best friend drew a decidedly physical response from deep inside her that she wasn't expecting.

She pulled herself out of the romantic fog she'd let herself slip into accidentally. "Are you really okay with this?" she asked.

"No," he said, ever honest, "but I'm going to do it anyway. For you."

She leaned in to hug him again and spoke softly into his ear. "Thank you for being the best friend a girl could ever have. I owe you big-time."

Kal chuckled, a low rumble that vibrated against her chest and made her want to snuggle closer to him. "Oh, you have no idea."

* * *

The Baby Proposal
is part of Mills & Boon Desire's Nº1 bestselling series, Billionaires and Babies: Powerful men...
wrapped around their babies' little fingers.

THE BABY PROPOSAL

BY
ANDREA LAURENCE

First Published in Great Britain 2016
By Mills & Boon, an imprint of HarperCollins*Publishers*
1 London Bridge Street, London, SE1 9GF

© 2016 Andrea Laurence

ISBN: 978-0-263-06597-8

Our policy is to use papers that are natural, renewable and recyclable
products and made from wood grown in sustainable forests. The logging
and manufacturing processes conform to the legal environmental
regulations of the country of origin.

Printed and bound in Great Britain
by CPI Antony Rowe, Chippenham, Wiltshire

Andrea Laurence is an award-winning author of contemporary romances filled with seduction and sass. She has been a lover of reading and writing stories since she was young. A dedicated West Coast girl transplanted into the Deep South, she is thrilled to share her special blend of sensuality and dry, sarcastic humor with readers.

To My Dancing Queens

Theresa, Jaime, Lucretia & Amanda

Thanks for all the girls' nights, the Soul Train dance parties, beach time and laughs. I'm not going to thank you for the tequila. Tequila is the devil. Even the good stuff.

One

Showtime.

The rhythmic sound of the drums pounded in the distance. On cue, one spotlight, then another, lit up the stage at the center of the open courtyard. With loud whoops and cries, the Mau Loa Maui dancing troupe took the stage.

Kalani Bishop watched the show begin from the dark corner of the courtyard. Spread out across the lawn of his resort were hundreds of hotel guests. They were mesmerized, as was Kal, by the beautiful movements of the traditional Hawaiian dancers onstage. He had no doubt that he had the finest traditional dancers on the entire island of Maui. He could have nothing less at his hotel.

The Mau Loa Maui had been the brainchild of Kal and his younger brother, Mano. Their family hotel, the original Mau Loa, was located on Waikiki Beach on Oahu. Growing up, they had dreamed of one day not only taking over the Oahu location but expanding the resort chain to other islands. First—Ka'anapali Beach in Maui. Kal had fallen in love with the island the moment he arrived. It was so different from Oahu— so lush and serenely beautiful. Even the women were more sensual, in his opinion, like ripe fruits waiting for him to pick them.

It was without question the most beautiful hotel on the island. The look on his grandparents' faces when they arrived at the resort the first time was proof enough that they approved of his work. The tourists certainly did. Since they opened, the resort had remained at capacity and had reservations booked solid a year in advance. They made vacation fantasies come true.

Part of the Hawaiian fantasy included attending an authentic luau with the kind of dancing seen in movies. At the Mau Loa Maui, the luau took place three nights a week and included a full dinner of kalua pork, poi, fresh pineapple, mango rice and other traditional Hawaiian foods. The guests sat on pillows around low tables that surrounded the stage.

Kal had worked hard to craft the perfect atmosphere for this hotel. Flames leaped from torches stationed around the wide lawn, lighting the area now that the sun had finally set into the sea beyond the stage. The fire cast shadows that flickered across the faces of the dancers and the musicians who beat drums and chanted along with them.

One of the female dancers took center stage. Kal smiled as his best friend, Lanakila Hale, commanded the attention of every person in the courtyard. Before she even began her solo dance performance, she had captivated the audience with her traditional Hawaiian beauty. She had long, wavy black hair that flowed over her golden brown skin. A crown of Plumeria flowers sat atop her head and circled her wrists and ankles. She was wearing a skirt made of long, green ti leaves that showed the occasional flash of her upper thighs and a bright yellow fabric top that bound her full breasts, leaving her stomach bare to highlight her toned core.

He couldn't help admiring her figure. They were friends, but it was impossible to ignore that Lana had an amazing dancer's body. It was hard, sculpted and lean after years and years of professional dance training. While she specialized in traditional Hawaiian dance, she had studied dance at the University of Hawaii and was well versed in almost every style including ballet, modern dance and hip-hop.

As the drums continued to beat faster, Lana kicked her movements into high gear. Her hips gyrated and swayed to the rhythm as her arms moved gracefully to tell the story of that particular hula dance. The hula wasn't just entertainment for tourists; it was his culture's ancient storytelling method. She was amazing, even better than she had been the night he first saw her dance in nearby Lahaina and knew he wanted her at his new hotel as the head choreographer.

Lana was the human embodiment of contradiction. She was both an athlete and a lady: strong and feminine, hard and yet with womanly curves in abundance. He couldn't imagine a more physically perfect specimen of a woman. She was an amazing person, too.

Smart, quick-witted, talented and not afraid to call him on his crap, which he needed from time to time.

He turned away to focus on the crowd as he felt his body start to react to her physical display. He didn't know why he tortured himself by watching the show when he knew what it would lead to. With each beat of the drum and thrust of her hips, his muscles tensed and his pulse sped up.

Kal reached up to loosen his tie and take a deep breath to wish away his attraction to Lana. It happened more often than he'd like where she was concerned, but who could blame him?

She might be his best friend, but she was undeniably his type. She was every red-blooded male's type, but she specifically checked every one of his boxes. *If* he had a list, and he didn't, because Kal didn't do relationships. Even if it wouldn't damage their friendship—and it would—there were other issues at play. Namely that he wasn't interested in the family and the white picket fence, and of course, Lana wanted the whole shebang more than anything. He couldn't risk sampling the forbidden fruit because she'd want him to buy the whole fruit basket. Giving in to his attraction for her could be a disaster, because if she wanted more and he didn't, where did that leave them?

Former best friends.

That wasn't an option, so they were to be friends and nothing more. He just wished he could convince his erection of that. They'd been friends for over three years now and he'd been unsuccessful so far. That meant the occasional cold shower to keep things in check, but he was managing.

The other female dancers joined Lana after her solo

to complete the routine. That was a helpful distraction. When they were finished, the male dancers took the stage and the ladies made a quick exit to change into their next dance costume. At the Mau Loa, the show went through the whole history of hula, covering years of styles and dress as it evolved. Kal didn't just want some cheesy performance to entertain the hotel guests; he wanted them to learn and appreciate his people and their culture.

"Do we meet with your approval, boss man?" a woman's voice asked from beside him.

Kal didn't have to turn to recognize Lana's low, sultry voice. He glanced to his left and found her standing beside him. As the choreographer, she did some dancing and filled in for ill or absent performers, but she didn't participate in the majority of the numbers herself.

"Some of you do," he noted, turning away from the show to focus all his attention on her. To be honest, the only dancer who could truly hold his interest was standing right beside him. "Alek is looking a little off tonight."

Lana's head snapped around to the stage and she narrowed her gaze at the performers. She watched the male dancer with her ever-critical eye. "I think he's a little hungover. I heard him talking to one of the other dancers about some wild night in Paia during practice this afternoon. I'll talk to him in the morning. He knows better than to mess around the night before a performance."

That was one of the reasons that Kal and Lana were such good friends. They both had a drive for perfection in all they did, Lana even more so than Kal. Kal liked everything to be just so, and he enjoyed his success, but he also enjoyed his play time. Lana was superfocused all the time, and really, she had to be to get to where she had in life. Not everyone could pull themselves up from poverty and turn their life into exactly what they'd wanted. It took drive and she had it in spades.

Sometimes he liked to point out faults just to watch her head spin like a top. Her cheeks would flush red, her nostrils would flare and her breasts would heave against her tight little tops in anger. It didn't help lessen his attraction to her, but it certainly made things more interesting.

"Everyone else looks great, though," he added to soothe her. "Good job tonight."

Lana crossed her arms over her chest and bumped her shoulder into his. She wasn't the most physically affectionate kind of person, never one to hang on other people. A bounce off the shoulder or a fist bump was about all she was comfortable with unless she was upset. When something was bothering her, all she wanted was a hug from Kal. He'd happily hold her until she felt better, enjoying what little affection she was willing to share.

The rest of the time, Lana was a no-nonsense kind of woman. He was actually kind of glad he wasn't one of her dancers. He'd seen her drill them in rehearsals, accepting nothing less than the perfection she herself was willing to give.

He was pretty sure that friends or no, if he ever got fresh he'd earn a stinging slap across the face. He liked that about her. Most of the local women he encountered on Maui knew exactly who he was. That meant they also knew exactly what he was worth. Like flies to honey, they'd do whatever he wanted to get close to him. He liked Lana with her tart vinegar to break up the sweetness from time to time.

The stage went dark and silent for a moment, catching both their attention. When the lights came back on, the men were gone and the ladies were returning to the stage in their long grass skirts, coconut bras and large headdresses. Kal lovingly referred to this routine as "the bootie shaker." He had no idea how the women moved as quickly as they did.

"There's a good crowd tonight," Lana noted.

"We always sell out on Sunday nights. Everyone knows this is the best luau in Maui."

Lana's dark gaze flicked over him and returned to the stage. Kal was bored with the dancing and instead focused on her. A light breeze carried the fragrance of her Plumeria flowers along with the sweet smell of her cocoa butter lotion to his nose. He drew it into his lungs, enjoying the scent that reminded him so much of nights laughing on the couch and sharing platters of sushi.

They spent a lot of their free time together. Kal dated periodically, as did Lana, but it never went anywhere. Him, by choice. Lana, because she had horrible taste in men. He loved her, but she was a loser magnet. She'd never get the husband and family she wanted with the kind of men she spent her time dating. That meant they spent a lot of time together. Kal's family was all on Oahu. Lana's family just wasn't worth the effort. Occasionally she would go visit her sister, Mele, and baby niece, Akela, but she always came back to the resort in a surly mood.

Thinking of family and free time jogged his memory. "Do you have plans for Christmas?" he asked. It was less than a month away, but the time would go by quickly.

"Not really," Lana answered. "You know it's so busy around here at Christmas. I've got the musicians working on some Christmas songs to do caroling, and we're adding a new holiday dance medley to the luau next week, which means extra rehearsals. I wouldn't ever presume to ask for time off around the holidays. What about you?"

Kal chuckled. "I'll be here, of course, helping guests celebrate Christmas at their tropical home away from home. Shall we carry on our annual holiday tradition of Christmas Eve sushi by my new fireplace while we exchange gifts?"

Lana nodded. "Sounds like a plan."

Kal was relieved. He didn't know what he would do if Lana ever found the man of her dreams. If she were to fall in love, start a family and build a life outside the Mau Loa, he would be all by himself. She'd been at his side since they broke ground on the hotel and he'd gotten used to her always being there.

Finding out his brother was engaged and expecting a baby with his fiancée made the worry crop up in his mind lately. His brother, Mano, had been fairly dedicated to not getting seriously involved with a woman, and yet Paige had gotten under his skin. Before he knew what hit him, he was in love. Kal didn't expect anything like that to ever happen to him—he was too stubborn to let anyone get that close.

But Lana...she deserved more than sushi with him on Christmas Eve. She deserved the life and family she wanted. He knew her childhood sucked. She wouldn't say as much, but he knew that having a family of her own was her way of building what she'd never had. He'd just have to find an outlet for his loneliness and jealousy when she was gone.

He glanced over and noticed Lana was leaning against the wall. She looked tired. "Are you okay?" he asked.

"Yeah," she said as she stared intently at the stage. "It's just been a long day. I'm going to go back to my room and change. Are you up for a late dinner after the show?"

"I am." Kal nodded in agreement. He actually couldn't remember when he'd eaten last. He could lose himself in work so easily.

"I'll meet you at the bar in half an hour. Let me know how the show goes."

"You've got it."

Lanakila made her way upstairs to her suite in the farthest corner of the hotel. It was, for all intents and purposes, her home. Kal had recently completed the construction of his private residence on the other side of the Mau Loa golf course. The sprawling home had taken quite a while to complete with its four bedrooms, large gourmet kitchen, three-car garage and tropical pool oasis in the backyard. Prior to that, he'd been living in a suite in the hotel so he could oversee every detail of operations.

Once he moved out into his new home, he'd opted to let Lana stay in his suite instead of remodeling it for a hotel room. She used to keep a small studio apartment up the coast in Kahakuloa, but she gave it up and sold all her furniture when she moved into the hotel. She stayed late most nights at the resort and was usually too exhausted to bother with the long drive home, so it was perfect.

It was actually bigger than her studio apartment had been anyway, and had a view of the ocean. She opened the door with her key card and slipped inside. Lana turned on the light in the tiny kitchenette before continuing through the living room into the bedroom. There, she slipped out of her costume and put her regular clothes back on.

She didn't like wandering around the hotel in her dance clothes. It made her feel like a character in a Hawaiian theme park or something. Besides that, she could tell it made Kal uncomfortable when she wasn't fully dressed. He averted his eyes and shifted nervously, something he never did when she was in street clothes.

Lana supposed that if Kal walked around in the men's dance costume all the time, it would make her uncomfortable, too, although for different reasons. The men danced in little more than a skirt of ti leaves. She had a hard enough time focusing on Kal's words when he was fully dressed in one of his designer suits. They covered every inch of his tanned skin, but they fit him like a glove and left little to the imagination.

Kalani Bishop was the most amazing specimen of male she'd ever laid her eyes on, and she'd gone to dance school, so that was saying something. And yet that was all she'd say on the subject. Longing for Kal was like longing for a pet tiger. It was beautiful and, if handled properly, could be a loving companion. But it was always wild. No matter what, you could never domesticate it. As much as she liked to live dangerously from time to time, she knew Kal was a beast well out of her league.

Clad in a pair of jeans and a tank top, she returned to the living room and picked up her phone where she'd left it during the performance. She noticed a message on her screen showing a missed call and a voice mail message from the Maui Police Department. Her stomach sank. Not again.

With her evermore violent father and her older sister, Mele, always getting into trouble, a call from the police station was not as rare as she'd like it to be.

Her mother had died when Lana was still a toddler. Their father, at least so she was told, had been a good man before that, but lost it when she died. He struggled after that, both in caring for his two young daughters and in coping with the loss. He turned to the bottle, a habit that released his temper. He'd never hit Lana or Mele, but he would shout the house down. He was also prone to getting in fights at the bar and getting arrested.

Lana had done everything right in an attempt to keep her father happy. That was how she got into dancing. Despite everything, her father was a proud Hawaiian man who believed they should honor their culture. Lana started taking hula as a child and continued into high school. Her father had never looked at her with as much pride as he did when he watched her dance.

Mele hadn't been as concerned. In her mind, she was going to be in trouble no matter what, so she might as well have some fun. That included dating every boy she could find except for the native Hawaiian ones whom their father would've approved of. When she finally did start dating a Hawaiian, he was nothing to get excited about. Tua Keawe was a criminal in the making. Mele met him while he was hustling tourists, and he only escalated his illegal activities from there. Lana stopped visiting her sister when she was home from college because Mele was always high or drunk.

Last year, Mele had found out she was pregnant and she really seemed to clean up her act. Lana's niece, Akela, was born free of addiction or side effects from fetal alcohol syndrome. She was a perfect, beautiful bundle that Lana adored more than anything. She'd always wanted a daughter of her own. Sometimes she wished the little girl was hers and not Mele's, if just for Akela's sake. Mele's model behavior hadn't lasted long past her delivery. She slipped back into her old habits, but there wasn't much Lana could do about it without risking Child Services taking the baby away.

One thing Lana had never confided in Kal about was her sister and her criminal lifestyle. He knew about her father, and that her sister was prone to get in trouble, but she tried to keep Mele's arrests under wraps. It was embarrassing, for one thing, to tell him. She knew he would understand and not judge her for their actions, but he was part of such an important and well-respected family. She was…not. Lana tried to pretend that she wasn't from poor trash most of the time, but her family always saw fit to remind her.

Lana also avoided the topic because she was always hoping that Mele would grow up and start acting like the older, responsible sister she was supposed to be. So far her hopes for a big sister she could rely on instead of keep an eye on hadn't materialized. Instead she leaned on Kal to be her responsible older sibling. She could go to him for advice and he would help her in any way he could.

Glancing at the screen, Lana worried that this time would be the one that her family had gotten into a mess that even Kal couldn't help her clean up. It was coming sooner or later. She finally worked up the nerve to hit the button on her phone and listen to the message.

"Lana, this is Mele. Tua and I got arrested. I need you to come get us out of here. This whole thing is just a load of crap. It was entrapment!" she shouted. "Entrapment!" she repeated, most likely to the officer nearby.

The line went dead and Lana sighed. It sounded like she was going to spend another night waiting to pay her sister's bail. Before she drove over there in the middle of the night, however, she was going to call the station. It had been a couple hours since her sister's message and she wanted to make sure she was still there.

She pressed the key to call back the police station. The switchboard operator answered.

"Yes, this is Lana Hale. I received a call from my sister, Mele Hale, about bail."

There was a moment of silence as the woman looked something up in the computer. "Yes, ma'am, please hold while I transfer you to the officer at the holding desk."

"This is Officer Wood," a man answered after a few moments.

"This is Lana Hale," she repeated. "I got a call from my sister about coming to bail her out. I wanted to check before I came down there so late."

The officer made a thoughtful noise before he answered. "Yes, your sister and her boyfriend were arrested today for possession of narcotics with intent to distribute. Apparently they attempted to sell heroin to an undercover police officer."

Lana bit back a groan. This was worse than she thought. She hadn't realized her sister had moved up from pot and LSD to a higher class of drug felony. "How much is her bail?" she asked.

"Actually your sister was misinformed when she called. There's no bail set for either of them. They're being held until tomorrow. Miss Hale will be meeting with a court-appointed attorney Monday morning prior to going before the judge."

That wasn't good. It sounded like their constant run-ins with the police were catching up with them. "Which judge?"

"I believe they're scheduled to see Judge Kona."

This time, the groan escaped Lana's lips before she could stop it. Judge Kona was known for being a hard nut. He was superconservative, supertraditional and he didn't tolerate any kind of crap in his courtroom. It wouldn't be Mele's first time before Judge Kona, and that wasn't good news. He didn't take kindly to repeat offenders.

A sudden thought popped into Lana's mind, making her heart stop in her throat. "What about their daughter?" Her niece, Akela, was only six months old. Hopefully they hadn't left her sleeping in her crib while they ran out to make a few bucks. It certainly wouldn't surprise Lana if they had.

"The baby was in the car, asleep in her car seat,

when the drug deal went down. She's been taken by Child Protective Services."

Panic made Lana's chest tight even though she knew her niece was technically safe. "No!" she insisted. "What can I do? I'll take her. She doesn't need to go to be with strangers."

"I understand how you feel," Officer Wood said, "but I'm afraid you'll have to wait and petition the judge for temporary guardianship while the legal guardians are incarcerated. In the meantime, the child will be placed in foster care. I assure you the baby will be well looked after. Perhaps more so than she was with her own parents."

Lana's knees gave out from under her and she sank down onto the couch. The rest of the call went quickly and before she knew it, the officer had hung up and she was staring blankly at her black phone screen.

She turned it back on to look at the time. It was late on a Sunday night. She'd have to wait to contact an attorney. Akela would be in foster care overnight no matter what, but if Lana had anything to say about it, she'd be with her by Monday afternoon.

It was a scary thought to leap unexpectedly into motherhood—she was completely unprepared—and yet she would do it gladly. Mele could be going to jail for months or years. Lana wouldn't be watching Akela overnight or for a weekend this time. She would be her guardian for however long it took for Mele to serve her debt to society.

She would need help to pull this off. Lana didn't want to do it, but she knew she had to tell Kal about what happened. Maybe he knew an attorney who would be better for Mele than the public defender or at the very least help her get guardianship of Akela.

Getting up from the couch, she slipped her phone into her back pocket and headed out to the bar to meet Kal. If anyone could help her out of this mess, it was him.

Two

Kal sat back in the chair at his lawyer's office the next day trying to keep quiet. They weren't here about him. They were here for Lana and Akela. Still, it was difficult to keep his mouth shut about the whole thing.

Lana had met him at the bar late last night, her eyes wild with panic. He'd never seen her like that. He'd forced a shot down her throat, sat her in a chair and made her tell him everything. Until that moment, he hadn't realized exactly how much Lana had kept from him about her family. He knew her father was a mess, but it seemed her sister was even worse. The thought of Lana's little niece being with strangers had made his blood boil. He'd only met her once, when Lana had her for an afternoon, but she was adorable, with chubby cheeks, long eyelashes and a toothless grin. Lana had been a fool for that baby, and now the baby was in trouble.

He'd called his attorney right then. When you had a six-figure retainer with Dexter Lyon, you got his personal number and permission to call him whenever you needed him. While Kal had never personally had a reason to summon his attorney from bed in the middle of the night, Lana did, and that was what mattered. He agreed to see them first thing Monday morning.

"It doesn't look good to be honest," Dexter said.

"What do you mean?" Lana said. Her face was flushed red and had been since the night before. She seemed to be on the verge of tears every second.

"I mean Judge Kona is a hard-ass. Yes, it absolutely makes sense for you to get custody of your niece. But let me tell you why he'd turn your petition down." Dexter looked at his notepad. "You're a dancer. You live out of a hotel room. You keep crazy hours. You're single. While none of those make you legally unfit to have children, adding them all together makes you a hard sell to the judge."

Lana frowned. "Well, for one thing, I'm a choreographer. I do stay in the hotel for convenience, but I can get an apartment if that's what it takes. I am single, but I can afford day care while I'm at work."

"And at night?" Dexter's brow went up curiously. "I'm just playing devil's advocate here. Judge Kona will ask these questions, so it's best you be prepared for them."

"I just don't understand how Lana can be considered unfit when the baby's actual parents are drug dealers. Even if she was an exotic dancer that lived in a van down by the river, she'd be more fit than Mele and Tua." Kal was getting mad. He wasn't used to being told no, especially when he called Dexter. Dexter was supposed to fix things. His reluctance to handle this made Kal more irritated by the second.

The attorney held up his hands in surrender. "I get it. I do. And I've gone ahead and filed for temporary guardianship. We're on the judge's docket for Wednesday."

"Wednesday!" Lana looked heartbroken. Kal imagined that if his niece was with strangers, he wouldn't want an hour to go by, much less a few days.

"There is no such thing as 'hurry' in the court system. We're lucky we got in Wednesday. Look at this time as the opportunity it is."

"Opportunity?" Lana repeated, skeptically.

"Yes. You've got two days to make yourself more fit. Find a place to live. Arrange for a nanny. Buy a crib. If you've got a serious boyfriend, marry him. All of that will help the cause."

Marry him? "Now, wait just a second," Kal said. He couldn't be quiet about this any longer. "You're recommending she just run out and marry someone so she can get custody?"

"Not just anyone. But if she's with someone serious, it's a great time to make the leap."

Lana sat back in her chair and dropped her head into her hands. "Just the way I'd always pictured it."

Kal didn't like seeing her like this. She looked totally defeated. He wasn't about to let her feel that way. "That's a nice idea, Dexter, but not everyone is in a relationship that can go to the next level on a day's notice."

Dexter shrugged. "Well, I figured it was a long shot, but it certainly wouldn't hurt. Focus your energies on an apartment and a caregiver, then. A nice place too. A studio isn't any better than a suite at a hotel." He stood and walked around his desk to lean against it. "I know that it seems like a lot of changes just for a temporary guardianship, but your sister and her boyfriend are in a lot of trouble. It might not be as temporary as you expect it to be.

"Life will get really complicated in a cramped apartment with a small baby after the first few weeks. My house is three thousand square feet, and when we brought our son home from the hospital, it felt like a tiny cardboard box. Baby crap everywhere. Everything is complicated by a factor of ten at least. It takes twenty minutes just to load up the car to run to the grocery store."

Lana groaned aloud. "Are you trying to talk me out of doing this?"

Dexter's eyes widened. "No, of course not. Kids are great. We have four now. My point is that I need you to do whatever you can to make it an easier transition. I have every intention of winning the motion Wednesday. I just need your help to make it impossible for the judge to say no. Every little thing you do can help."

A soft knock came at the door.

"Yes?" Dexter asked loudly.

His assistant poked her head inside. "I'm sorry, Mr. Lyon, but Mr. Patterson is on line two and he's very upset. He refuses to speak to anyone but you."

Dexter looked at Lana, then at Kal. "Do you mind if I take this call in the other room? It should only take a minute."

Kal nodded and Dexter slipped out the door with his assistant. He couldn't shake the irritation that furrowed his brow. He didn't like any of this and he certainly didn't like this judge. Who was he to impose his value system on others? Lana shouldn't have to rearrange her whole life for this. There was nothing wrong with the way she lived. She wasn't a drug dealer or a heroin addict, so she was a step above her sister as a fit guardian, easily.

He wanted to say something, but Lana's pensive expression gave him pause. He didn't want to interrupt her. She got the same look on her face when she was working out a dance routine. The whole thing would play out in her mind like a film as she thought it through. If you spoke to her, she'd have to start over from the beginning.

Finally her brown eyes came into focus and she turned to look at him. Her dark hair was pulled into a ponytail today that swung over her shoulder as she moved. While her long, thick hair was beautiful and he often fantasized about running his fingers through it, he knew it annoyed the hell out of her. She kept it long for the show, but if she wasn't performing, it was usually pulled back from her face. Thankfully that relieved the temptation. Most of the time.

"So I've got an idea," she said. "It's a little out there, so do me a favor and just go with it for a second."

He didn't know that he liked the sound of that. It usually meant trouble where she was concerned. "Okay."

She held out her hands to count her points on her fingers. "So, obviously my job isn't going to change and there's no reason that it should."

"Agreed."

"I can find a day care for the days I work with the dancers and a babysitter for the nights of the luau."

"That's true. I can also give you some time off, you know. I think you have about two hundred hours' worth of vacation you've never used."

Lana frowned at him. She seemed to be doing a lot of that lately, and he didn't like it. He wanted to reach out and rub away the crease between her eyebrows and kiss the pout of her lips until she smiled again. Or hit him. As long as she stopped looking so upset. Instead he kept his hands and mouth to himself.

"While that's a nice idea, it's Christmas. We're super busy. There's no way I'm taking off the whole month. Besides, if what your lawyer says is true and I have Akela longer than a month or two, I'm going to need my leave for when she's sick or has doctor's appointments. No one I know with kids under the age of three has any personal leave accrued, especially if the child goes to day care. They catch all the bugs there."

Kal hadn't really thought about that. If this did turn into a long-term arrangement, Akela would take up a huge portion of her time. He felt a pang of jealousy at the idea that he might be losing his best friend for a while. He totally understood, but he wondered what he would do while she was consumed by caring for her niece. "Okay. I just wanted to let it be known that your boss says it's all right if you have to do it."

Lana nodded. "Thanks. He's usually a jerk, so I'm glad he can be reasonable about this." She grinned for the first time since she'd gotten the call from her sister, and he felt a sense of relief wash over him at last. That smile gave him a little hope, even if it was at his expense.

"A bigger apartment in Maui...now, that's a hard one. I can't afford anything like that on the west side

of the island. And if I move any farther east, the com-
mute will be awful."

Real estate in Maui really was ridiculous. He tried
not to think about how much he'd paid for the land his
hotel sat on. There were so many zeroes in that check
that he had a hard time signing it and he *had* the money.
He couldn't imagine trying to live here on an average
income. Lana made good money, but she didn't make
beachfront condo money.

He'd forgotten her old apartment was so small. She'd
noted how big the hotel suite was when she moved in,
so he should've considered that. It felt tiny to him now
that he was living in such a huge house. *Huge house…*
that was a thought.

"What about moving in with me?" He spat the words
out before really thinking them through.

Lana looked at him, narrowing her almond-shaped
eyes. "That would help a lot, actually. Are you sure,
though? It's going to be a major cramp on your bach-
elorhood to have me and a baby in the house."

Kal shrugged that off. He rarely had time for anything aside from work this time of year. Plus, if Lana
was in the house with the baby, he wouldn't miss out
on his time with her. He'd never admit to his selfish
motivations, however. "I've got three extra bedrooms
just sitting empty. If it will help, I'm happy to do what
I can."

Lana beamed at him. "I'm actually really glad you
said that, because I was just about to get to the crazy
part of my plan."

Kal swallowed hard. She had something in mind
that was crazier than moving in together with a baby?

Just then Lana slid off of her chair and onto one

knee in front of him. She took his hand and held it as he frowned down at her. "What are you doing?" he asked as his chest grew tight and he struggled to breathe. His hand was suddenly burning up where she held him in hers, the contact lighting his every nerve on fire. He wanted to pull away and regain control of himself, but he knew he couldn't. This was just the calm before the storm.

Lana took a deep breath and looked up at him with a hopeful smile. "I'm asking you to marry me."

Lana looked up at Kal and anxiously waited for his answer. The idea had just come to her and she acted on it before she lost her nerve. It was crazy, she knew that, but she was willing to do whatever it took to get guardianship of Akela. So now here she was, on one knee, proposing marriage to her best friend, who had no interest in ever marrying.

Judging by the panic-stricken expression on Kal's face, this wasn't what he was expecting and he didn't want to say yes. She clutched his hand tighter in hers, noting that his touch strengthened her even when he'd much rather pull away. He was her support, her ideal, her everything. This could work. It had to.

"I'm sorry I don't have a diamond ring for you," she started rambling in the hopes of breaking the tension in the room. "I wasn't planning on getting engaged today."

Kal didn't laugh. His eyes just grew wider as he subtly shook his head in disbelief. "Are you serious?" he asked.

"Dead serious. You just said you were happy to do whatever you could to help me get Akela. If we're married and living together in your big house when we go into court on Wednesday, there's no way the judge will turn down the request."

Kal leaned forward and squeezed her hands. "You know I would do anything for you. But married? I never… I mean…that's kind of a big deal."

The fact that Kal hadn't flat-out said no to this whole thing made her love him even more. "It doesn't have to be a big deal," she argued. "Listen, I know how you feel about marriage, and I get it. I'm not asking you to stay with me forever or fall madly in love with me. We're not going to sleep together or anything. That would be crazy talk. I just want this marriage to be for show. We spend so much time together that no one would find it suspect that we've quietly fallen in love and eloped. It's the perfect cover. We get married, stay married as long as we need to to make the judge and Child Services happy. Then we annul it or divorce or whatever when it's all done. At most, you'll have to kiss me a couple times in public. That shouldn't be too horrible, right?"

A flicker of what looked like disappointment crossed Kal's face for a moment. Lana wasn't sure what that was about. It wasn't possible that he might relish the idea of them being man and wife. The thought alone sent a thrill through Lana that she refused to acknowledge, but it was all obligation on his part, she was certain.

After a moment, he took a deep breath and then he nodded. "So we get married, move you into my place and play the happy couple for the general public until Akela can safely return to her parents. That's it?"

Lana nodded. "That's it, I promise. If you so much

as try anything more than that, I'll be sure to give you a good slap to remind you who you're dealing with."

That, finally, brought a smile to Kal's face. She breathed a sigh of relief, knowing that he was going to go along with her harebrained plan even though it involved a major life milestone that he never expected to achieve with the kind of woman he'd never lower himself to love.

"So, Kalani Bishop, would you do me the honor of being my fake husband?" she asked again, since he hadn't truly responded the first time.

He pressed his lips together for a moment, and then he finally nodded. "I guess so."

"Yay!" Lana leaped into his arms and hugged him close. She buried her nose in his neck, drawing in the scent of his cologne. The familiar musk of her best friend drew a decidedly physical response from deep inside her that she wasn't expecting with everything else that was going on. Her heart started racing in her chest as she held his spicy male scent in her lungs and enjoyed his arms wrapped tightly around her. No one held her like he did, and there was no one she wanted to hold her more than Kal.

Then she felt him stiffen awkwardly against her. She pulled herself out of the romantic fog she'd let herself accidentally slip into. This wasn't the reaction of someone who was comfortable with his decision. She drew back and looked at the lines on his face that reflected conflict and shame instead of excitement and confidence. Lana needed to remember that this was all for show. It might be her innermost secret fantasy coming to life, but he was only doing this for her because it was important and they were friends, not for any other reason. She needed to save her physical reactions to him for public consumption or she'd scare him off.

"Are you really okay with this?" she asked.

"No," he said, ever honest, "but I'm going to do it anyway. For you."

His words nearly brought tears to her eyes. She leaned in to hug him again and spoke softly into his ear. "Thank you for being the best friend a girl could ever have. I owe you big-time."

Kal chuckled, a low rumble that vibrated against her chest and made her want to snuggle closer to him. "Oh, you have no idea."

The door of the room opened again and Lana pulled away from Kal to turn to Dexter. "We're getting married," she announced before he could change his mind.

Dexter looked at Lana, then curiously at Kal and his pained expression. "Excellent. Shall I draw up a prenup? I presume that assets won't comingle, and everyone keeps what they have going into the union?"

"Sure," Lana said. Part of her thought that Kal might balk at the idea of a prenuptial agreement, but she wanted him to have that protection. She didn't want any of his stuff and she wanted to make sure he knew it. "I don't want him getting his hands on my old-school hi-fi system."

Kal turned to look at her. "Your what?"

"It has a turntable. Records are cool again."

He just shook his head. "Draw something up and we'll come back to sign it in the morning. We'll get married tomorrow afternoon assuming the wedding pavilion at the hotel isn't booked. That should be good enough for the judge, right?"

"The two of you married and living in that big new

house…oh yeah." Dexter nodded enthusiastically. "Then you'll just have to put on a good show for Child Services when they come for home visits. If you can pull this off, it will make my job ten times easier."

"Okay," Kal said, pushing up from his seat. "We'll see you in the morning, then." He reached out for Lana's hand, something he'd never done before. "Come on, *honey*. We've got a lot of plans to make if we're going to get married tomorrow afternoon."

Lana twisted her lips in amusement. The stiff way he said the words was proof enough that he was really uncomfortable with the situation but was too good of a friend to say no. She didn't say anything, though. Instead she took his hand and they walked out of the attorney's office together.

They were silent until they got back to the car. Kal had parked his F-type Jaguar convertible in the shade on the far side of the parking lot. Lana had always loved Kal's car. It was the kind of vehicle that motorheads fantasized about. Lana drove an old Jeep without doors, so this felt superluxurious. As she climbed in beside him and looked around this time, however, she realized they had an issue.

"Kal?"

"Yeah?" he asked as he started the engine and it roared to life.

"You drive a two-seater convertible and I drive a Jeep Wrangler without doors or a roof."

Kal pulled the car out of the parking lot and onto the main highway. "And?"

"And… I don't think we can put a car seat in either of those."

"Hmm," he said thoughtfully as they went down the

highway. "You're probably right. It's never something that's mattered before. I'll have someone bring a car over. I'll lease one for as long as we have Akela. What do you think is responsible enough? A minivan? An SUV with all the airbags? Or would you rather have a sedan of some kind?"

She hadn't really thought that far ahead, as evidenced by this predicament. "Not a minivan. That's all I ask. Other than that, as long as it has a backseat I can put a car seat in and will protect her from the elements, I think I'm good. Thank you."

"No problem." Kal looked past her toward the shopping center they were coming up on. "Since we're discussing the ways we're completely unprepared for marriage and parenthood, I think we need to make a pit stop."

Lana held on as he whipped the car into the parking lot and came to a stop outside a baby supercenter. She'd only set foot in it once, to buy a baby shower gift for Mele. "I don't know what we need yet. I've got to go by Mele's apartment and see what she has."

Kal shook his head and turned off the car. "No, you don't. We're getting all new stuff. Come on."

Lana leaped out of the car and jogged to catch up with him. "Are you serious? I can't afford to buy all new baby things."

Kal pulled his dark sunglasses down his nose to look at her with an expression that could've melted a woman's panties right off. Lana had learned early on that when he looked at *her* that way, it wasn't smoldering, it was irritation.

"You're not buying it. I am."

She suspected he might say that. "This is too much,

Kal," she complained. He simply ignored her, going into the store ahead of her. "Kal!" she finally shouted with her hands planted on her hips.

He stopped and turned around to look at her. "What is the problem?"

She narrowed her gaze at him. Women she'd had as friends over the years had asked her how she could be friends with a man as hot at Kal and not want more. While she convinced herself she didn't want more, she used this as exhibit number one: he was stubborn as an ox. "It's too much."

"We're already getting married and moving in together to pull this off. What is too much, exactly?"

She knew he was right. "I don't want you to buy a ton of things. We might only have her for a few weeks."

"Or we might have her for years. Either way, she needs a place to sleep, food, clothes, diapers... If it makes you happy, I'll donate everything to charity when we're done. It won't go to waste, okay?"

Lana bit at her bottom lip but knew she'd lost this battle before it started. Kal wasn't about to decorate the baby's nursery with the thrift store finds they collected from Mele's apartment. "Fine."

Inside the store, Kal waved his finger at the manager standing behind the customer service desk. "We're going to need some assistance."

The woman came forward, polite, but curious about his forwardness. "What can I help you with, sir?"

"With everything. We're buying it all, so I need someone to jot down what we choose as we go through the store and have it delivered to my home."

The manager seemed flustered but grabbed a clipboard and the registry scanner and went straight to leading him up and down the aisles. Lana tried not to roll her eyes. Why Kal couldn't just get a cart and shop like a normal person, she didn't know.

She figured it out soon, however. There wasn't a cart big enough. He hadn't been exaggerating when he said he was going to buy everything. It took about two hours to go through the entire store. They bought a complete bedroom suite with a crib, changing table, dresser, lamp and rocking chair. They got bedding, a mobile, a car seat, a high chair, a stroller and a swing. Diaper bags, bottles, cases of baby food and diapers, medicine, shampoo…you name it. They even bought about twenty outfits and pajamas.

It was exhausting, but Lana had to admit Kal had good taste. Everything he selected was beautiful. The furniture for the nursery was a soft gray color that complemented the star and moon bedding set. It was enchanting for a baby's room. Hopefully Akela would love all her new things as much as Lana did. She was so young, she probably couldn't appreciate most of it, but the toys Kal purchased last would be a big hit with the baby at least.

As they finished selecting the last few things, Lana took a step back and counted her blessings. There was no way she could make any of this happen without Kal. He was an amazing friend and person. Not just for agreeing to marry her, but for all of it.

She really didn't understand why Kal was determined to stay single. He insisted he was too busy for that sort of thing, but she didn't believe it. He was the kind of man who could make any dream into reality. If he wanted a family, all he had to do was snap his fingers and women would line up to volunteer for the job. He was tall and muscular with a build they would clamor to run their hands over. His hair was dark and wavy, and his skin was golden brown. His smile could melt her defenses. Honestly, when he was wearing one of his expensive suits and marching around the hotel like a man on a mission, she had a hard time figuring out why she didn't just throw herself at him.

She joked about what a pain he could be, how stubborn he was, what a playboy he was to go through women the way he did. The truth was far different. She loved Kal. He was the best thing in her life, where she didn't have much outside of her job and her friendship with him to rave about. If she really let herself think about it, she probably would want him. It was just a ridiculous thought, so she never let herself have it.

Kal was simply too good for her. He was educated, rich, cultured and from an important family. Yes, they could be friends and even fake husband and wife, but a real relationship with a woman like her? Even if he was open to marriage, he wouldn't choose her. She was really surprised he agreed to fake marry her considering her sister was in jail and her family was such a mess. Their friendship made it possible and she would cling to that for dear life. It was better than any romantic relationship, anyway.

It sure made dating hard, though. Where would she find a man to measure up to Kal? It was impossible, and she'd certainly tried. Over the last few years, she'd gone through a steady stream of losers. None even came close to Kal. Not only was he handsome and ridiculously rich, but he was funny, kind, thoughtful... She couldn't have chosen a better best friend. And come tomorrow, a better husband, even if just for show.

All she'd expected him to do was sign on the dotted line, hold her hand in court and act like a loving husband in public. Instead he was paying a small fortune, fully committing to making this work. All to make Lana happy.

Lana didn't know why Kal was single, but it was easy to see why she couldn't commit to someone else.

Three

Kal straightened the bow tie of his white tuxedo and looked himself over in the mirror. He certainly looked like a groom. He was as nervous as he imagined a groom would be. But that spark of excitement was missing. It just all felt awkward. Backward. Definitely not how he'd intended to spend his Tuesday.

Marriage hadn't always been an alien concept to Kal. When he was younger it was something he knew he would do someday, but reality intruded. When he was twenty, a car accident claimed the lives of his parents and left his brother blind. Kal realized then that no one was invincible, including him. He'd grown up so sheltered and privileged that he almost thought nothing bad could ever happen to him. Then, in an instant, he'd lost the most important people in his life. No warnings, no goodbyes, just gone forever.

Suddenly he had more responsibilities piled on him than most kids his age. His grandparents helped with the hotel while Kal finished college and Mano adjusted to his disability, but Kal eventually stepped up to lead the family when he graduated. That was enough family and responsibility for him. Marriage was not in the cards for Kal. He wasn't sure he could go through something like that again—getting attached to someone else just to lose her...or to leave a family behind to pick up the pieces after his death. It seemed like too much risk for the potential reward.

So why, then, was he pinning an orchid to his lapel and heading out the door to the Mau Loa's wedding pavilion? Well, because he just couldn't say no to Lana.

When she'd looked up at him, her dark brown eyes pleading with him to say yes...there was no question that he would do whatever she asked of him. He just wanted to make sure she was serious and set boundaries for this "marriage."

It wasn't that Lana wasn't beautiful. She was exactly his type. Therein lay the problem. The day they met, Kal knew she could very easily be the one to make him throw caution to the wind and fall in love. Since they had such different priorities for their futures, he knew better than to let that happen. Instead he'd placed her in the friend bucket. It was the smartest thing to do considering how important their friendship was to him and that she was technically his employee.

Knowing that Lana just wanted a wedding for show had been both a relief and a challenge for him. A part of him had always wondered if they would be as great together as a couple as they were as friends. He suspected so. Being this close, having to touch her and kiss her to keep up their public facade, and yet to still have to maintain that friendly distance when they were alone would be difficult. It was like letting himself have a single bite of his favorite dessert—just enough to whet his appetite, but not enough to satisfy him. It was easier to just avoid the dish entirely, especially when the dish was as sensual and tasty as Lana.

Giving himself one last glance in the mirror, Kal stepped out of his house and drove his Jaguar to the hotel. His home was on the far corner of the property, with a sprawling golf course separating it from the rest of the resort. Most days he would walk or take the golf cart, but it seemed wrong to have his new bride hop on a golf cart after their ceremony.

The wedding pavilion was right on the beach. The bright white gazebo had room for a wedding party of ten and seating for up to a hundred guests on the lawn in front of it. It was raised up, overlooking the ocean and surrounded by lush plants to give some privacy from the tourists sunbathing nearby.

Kal had built it because he thought it was good business. They didn't have room for one at the Waikiki location, so he'd been certain to reserve a place for it to be built here. Hawaii was a huge destination wedding locale and they needed to get in on the action. Not once had he ever thought he would use it for himself.

The traditional Hawaiian officiant, the kahuna *pule*, was already there, waiting under the pavilion to start the wedding. The short, round, older man with snow-white hair wore the traditional crown of *haku lei*. A small table in front of him was already set up with everything that was needed for the ceremony— the conch shell, the white orchid and green *maile* leis, and a wooden *Koa* bowl filled with ocean water and *ti* leaves to bless the rings.

Kal felt his breast pocket in a moment of panic and realized that he did remember the rings. Earlier that morning, they'd gotten their marriage license and taken care of all the legal details at Dexter's office. They'd then stopped at a jewelry store to select two simple but attractive wedding bands. Lana had insisted that he'd already spent too much already and flat-out refused a diamond. It felt odd not to buy one, although buying a wedding ring at all was odd enough.

All that was left was for the kahuna *pule* to perform the ceremony and sign the paperwork, and he and Lana were married. The thought sent a momentary surge of panic though him. He'd tried to suppress it the last few days, focusing on details and plans, but things were suddenly getting very real. Every step he took toward the pavilion made it even more so.

His family was going to kill him when they found out about this, especially Mano. His tūtū Ani would likely chew his ear off over the phone. He wished he could just keep it a secret, but since they had to play this relationship as real, he had to tell them. Dexter had warned that Child Services would not only come by the house but could conduct interviews with family and friends. That meant everyone needed to believe that they were husband and wife in every sense of the word. That seemed cruel to do to his family, as they waited anxiously for him to find a wife. Considering he would be divorcing in a short time and this was all a sham, he hated to get their hopes up for nothing. Hopefully he could get away with just telling Mano for now and wait to tell the rest of the family, if necessary, after the New Year.

"Aloha, Mr. Bishop," the Hawaiian holy man greeted him as he stepped up into the pavilion.

"Aloha and *mahalo*. I want to thank you for coming on such short notice."

The older man shook his head. "I always have time in my day to bring together a couple in love. Your hotel is one of my favorite places to perform ceremonies."

Kal felt a pang of guilt, but he knew he'd better get over it. This man was just the first of many they were lying to to get guardianship of Akela. "I appreciate that. I tried to build something our guests would be willing to travel to Maui to have."

"Do you have the rings?"

Kal reached into his breast pocket and pulled out the two wedding bands. "I do. Here they are."

"Very good. I will be ready to start whenever your bride arrives."

Kal looked down at his watch. They'd agreed on four in the afternoon. It was a minute till. He took a deep breath and tried not to be concerned about Lana's punctuality. Kal wasn't in a rush to marry anyway, but he did want this part to be over with quickly.

"Ah, there she is."

Kal turned to look in the direction the kahuna *pule* indicated and felt his heart go stone silent in his chest. It was like he'd hit a brick wall at full speed when he saw her. His whole body tightened when he took in his bride, and his tuxedo chafed at his collar and other un-mentionable places as though it had suddenly shrunk two sizes.

Lana looked…amazing.

Traditionally Hawaiian brides wore a flowing white dress that was cut in the style of a muumuu. He was extremely thankful at that moment that Lana had opted for something more modern and formfitting on the top. The white lace gown had a deep V neckline that accentuated her shapely décolletage and plunged all the way to the waist. There, the dress flowed down in soft layers of organza that moved in the breeze. Her hair was loose around her shoulders and she was wearing a traditional ring of haku flowers on her head.

Everything about her was soft, romantic and made him long for a wedding night he wasn't going to have. It was possible that Lana was the most beautiful bride in the history of brides. He couldn't take his eyes off her. Everything around them faded away as though she were all there was in the whole world. In fact, when the kahuna *pule* blew into the conch shell to announce the arrival of the bride and summon the elements to bear witness to the ceremony, Kal nearly leaped off the ground in surprise.

Lana grinned wide with rosy-pink lips as she walked up the path to him. He reached out to take her hand and help her up the stairs. Despite her joyful demeanor, her hands were ice-cold. He was relieved to know he wasn't the only nervous one.

"Are we ready to begin?" the holy man asked.

"Yes."

"Very well." The kahuna *pule* opened up his prayer booklet to the marked page. "The Hawaiian word for love is aloha. Today we've come together to celebrate the special aloha that exists between you, Kalani and Lanakila, and your desire to make your aloha eternal through the commitment of marriage. As you know,

the giving of a lei is an expression of aloha. Kal and
Lana, you will exchange leis as a symbol of your aloha
for each other. When two people promise to share the
adventure of life together, it is a beautiful moment that
they will always remember.

"Kal, please place the orchid lei around Lana's
neck."

Kal reached for the white orchid lei on the table,
and Lana tipped her head down for him to place it
over her shoulders.

"The unbroken circle of the lei represents your eternal commitment and devotion to each other. The beauty
of each individual flower is not lost when it becomes a
part of the lei, but is enhanced because of the strength
of its bond. Lana, would you place the maile leaf lei
around Kal's neck."

Kal watched as she took the long strand of green
leaves off the table. Her hands were trembling as she
lifted it over his head. He caught her eye and winked
to reassure her. They would get through this together
because that was what best friends did.

"Kal and Lana, you are entering into marriage because you want to be together. You are marrying because you know you will grow more in happiness and
aloha more fully as life mates. You will belong entirely to each other, one in mind, one in heart and in
all things. Now please hold hands and look into each
other's eyes."

Kal took her hands in his and held them tightly. He
didn't know if it was the situation or how beautiful she
looked today, but touching her was different than before. He felt an unexpected thrill as he took her hand,
and it raced all the way through his nervous system like

the burning fuse of a firecracker. He was suddenly very aware of the scent of the flowers in her hair, the subtle sparkle of her lipstick and the silky softness of her skin.

"Do you, Kalani, take Lanakila to be your wife? To have and to hold, from this day forward? For better or for worse, for richer or for poorer, in sickness and in health? To cherish with devoted love and faithfulness till death do you part?"

Kal swallowed hard and found his mouth so dry he could barely part his tongue from the roof of his mouth. He wasn't used to being nervous, but this had certainly done the trick. "I do," he managed at last.

That was the easy part. Now he just had to try to live up to the impossible vow he'd just taken.

The holy man repeated the vows for Lana, but she was hardly listening. How could she hear what he said over the loud pounding of her heart?

She'd been okay until the ceremony started. She'd had butterflies in her stomach, but she'd held it together as long as she focused on each little task—finding a dress, doing her hair, applying her makeup. In the mirror of her suite, she kept repeating to herself that this wasn't about love, this was about Akela. The ceremony itself was the only real part of this entire marriage. Perhaps that was the problem. As she stood here looking into Kal's dark brown eyes and let his warm hands steady her shaky ones, it felt real. Too real.

Lana let a ragged breath escape her lungs, then realized both men were looking expectantly at her. "I do," she said quickly, and hoped that was the correct response.

It was. The kahuna *pule* continued with the ceremony by blessing the wedding rings. He placed the ti leaf in the koa bowl that was filled with seawater. He then sprinkled the water three times over the ring and repeated the blessing before handing the smaller of the two rings to Kal.

Kal repeated the required words, all the while looking into Lana's eyes as though there were no other person on the whole planet. There was a twinkle of mischief there in his dark gaze that she recognized and appreciated. He was trying to calm her nerves by acting as though he wasn't nervous. She knew better. His right eyelid kept twitching. It hadn't done that since opening day of the resort.

"Lana, please place the ring on Kal's finger and repeat after me."

Lana slipped the platinum band onto Kal's finger and pledged to be with him until death. She squeezed her eyes shut for a moment and tried not to let the doubts creep in as the words left her lips. She only had seconds to change her mind and then she would legally be Mrs. Kalani Bishop.

It's not real, she repeated silently to herself as the kahuna *pule* continued to speak. She was not Kal's blushing bride, he wasn't in love with her and there would be no wedding night fantasy come to life tonight. Lana needed to shut down her brain and her libido before it was met with a great deal of disappointment.

"Lana and Kal," the kahuna *pule* continued, "you have pledged your eternal aloha to each other and your commitment to live together faithfully in lawful wedlock. By the authority vested in me by the laws of the state of Hawaii, I pronounce you husband and wife. Kal, you may kiss your bride."

And just like that, it was done.

With that worry aside, Lana suddenly had a new one. Kal was moving closer and the charade was about to get physical for the first time. Repeating vows was one thing, but the line between friend and lover was on the verge of being irrevocably blurred.

Kal's hand rested against her cheek and drew her lips closer to his. Lana's breath caught in her throat as the panic threatened to seize her. She vacillated between wanting this kiss more than she should, dreading it, and hoping they managed to convince the holy man it was authentic. With no other choice but to go through with this, she closed her eyes and tried to relax.

Half a heartbeat later, she felt Kal's lips against her own. They were soft and gentle as they pressed insistently to hers. Lana couldn't suppress the shiver that ran through her body or the prickle of energy that shot down her spine. She hadn't intended to, but she was having a genuine physical reaction to his kiss.

Before she could stop herself, she climbed to her toes to get closer to him. Her palms pressed against the massive wall of his chest. The scent of his cologne mingled with the tropical flowers and the warmth of his skin, and they all combined to draw her in.

Lana had never quite understood why women threw themselves at Kal when they couldn't keep him. Well, she understood he was handsome, charming and rich, but she watched as time after time they fell under his spell and lost all their good sense. She'd always thought that those women were silly. Yes, her best friend was a great catch, but he was also a blanket hog and he always ate the last piece of sushi. There was no reason to make a fool of themselves over him. Especially when he had no intention of taking their relationship much past the bedroom.

The bedroom.

Lana felt a pang of need deep inside her at the thought. No matter how often she reminded herself about how fake this all was, her body clearly ignored her. It had decided that she was married, so she would be getting a little action tonight from the tall, dark piece of man kissing her. Not so.

With her hands still pressed on his chest, she pushed back and ended the kiss. Certainly that was enough to satisfy the holy man and make this official. There was no need to go overboard, right?

When she looked up at Kal, he seemed affected by their kiss, as well. His dark eyes were glassy and dilated. His skin seemed a little more flushed than usual. Good. It wasn't just her. She'd feel like an idiot if she got all worked up over that simple kiss and he treated it like just another day at the races.

She expelled the air and his scent out of her lungs slowly and looked back toward the kahuna *pule* before she tried to kiss Kal again. This had all happened so fast she hadn't truly allowed herself to prepare, mentally, for the change in their friendship.

"Ho'omaika'i 'ana," the kahuna *pule* said with a wide smile across his face. "Congratulations to you both."

"Mahalo," Kal said, thanking him.

The next few minutes were a blur. They all signed the marriage license, making it truly official. Then the kahuna *pule* gathered up his things and was gone, leaving them alone in the pavilion. Man and wife.

Lana looked out at the ocean for a minute, waiting for the surreal feeling to pass. It wasn't going to. No matter how many times she pinched herself, she would still be married.

"That went well, I think."

Lana turned to look at Kal. He was standing with his hands shoved casually into his pockets, as though they hadn't just gotten married a moment before. He had the same smirk on his face as always.

"I suppose. We're married, so that was the most important part."

He sauntered over to where she was standing and eyed her with a curiously raised brow. "That kiss was pretty convincing."

More convincing than she'd anticipated. She didn't want to admit that to him, though. The potential for things to be awkward between them was high enough without that. "We're pretty good actors, aren't we?"

The smirk disappeared. Was he disappointed because he thought that he could nearly melt her knees out from under her? Lana could tell her best friend many things, but that wasn't one of them. She'd promised him this would just be for show and short term at that. If he knew he could turn her on without even trying, she'd never live that down. He still liked to remind her of the time she'd had too much to drink and groped his rear end.

"So, now what?" she asked.

Kal shrugged. "Well, I think normal people would go have some wild sex to make things official."

Lana's entire body clenched at the mere thought of it. What was wrong with her? This was never a problem before, but one little ceremony that wasn't supposed to mean anything had flipped some sort of switch inside her libido where Kal was concerned.

"Since that's off the table," he continued, "I say we change and go out to a celebratory dinner. While we're gone, I'll have your things packed up and moved to my place."

"So soon?" she asked. "I can pack my own stuff."

"I'm sure you can, but why would you? That's what I pay people for. You need to be all moved in and ready to go for tomorrow. If the judge sends some kind of social services worker to the house to check on everything and make sure we have a proper home for Akela, I don't want the place to be a mess of moving boxes."

He was right. Lana knew he was right.

"Come on. I'll give you a ride back to the hotel and you can change and grab a few things. Then someone will pack up the rest."

"You don't want to go out to dinner in our wedding finery?" she teased. She held out her dress and swayed a little to make the flowing fabric swirl around her. Having twenty-four hours to find a dress had made things difficult, but when she saw this one in the window of the bridal shop, she knew it was the one for her. Thankfully the cut didn't require alterations and she was able to buy the sample. She loved it.

And judging by the way Kal looked at her when she was walking up the path to the pavilion, he liked it, too. He'd stared at her so intensely she could almost feel his gaze on her bare skin.

"We could," he said, eyeing the low cut of the dress's bodice and clearing his throat uncomfortably. "I, uh, just thought you would be more comfortable. And I wouldn't want you to spill something on it."

Lana smiled. Finally he seemed as awkward as she did. She wouldn't mind wearing the dress out or changing; she just wanted to see him squirm. "You're right. I'll change. It's pretty, but it isn't very comfortable."

Kal nodded and reached his hand out to her. "Shall we go, then, Mrs. Bishop?"

She froze in her tracks at the sound of her married name. She tried to recover, reaching out to him. Her eyes fell on the shiny wedding band on her ring finger and followed it as it rested on his outstretched palm. *Mrs. Bishop.*

"Are you having second thoughts, Lana?"

She looked up at him with wide eyes. "What?"

Kal pulled her close to him and looked down at her. His eyes were lined with concern as he searched her face. "You look...troubled. I went along with this because it was what you wanted, but if you've changed your mind, we can rip up the license and pretend it never happened."

Part of her wanted to say yes. She felt she was dangling off a cliff and he was the only one who could snatch her back from the precipice. But she knew she couldn't. She had to do this for Akela.

"No," she said as firmly as she could. "This was the right thing to do. A little scary, but the right thing. Thank you for doing this for me."

Kal smiled and pulled her into a comforting hug. "For you, Lana...anything."

Four

They drove up the coast to have a celebratory sushi dinner at their favorite place in Kapalua. When they told their server they were there celebrating their wedding, she ran to the bakery next door and got them a vanilla cupcake to share, since they didn't serve desserts.

Lana felt guilty about the whole thing. Kal insisted they needed to celebrate and share the news with as many people as possible, but it bothered her. She hadn't really thought about the part of the plan where they had to lie to everyone about their relationship. Lying to the judge and the county employees didn't seem as bad as lying to their favorite waitress, their family or their friends.

When they got back to the house, Lana was amazed to find her things there and mostly put away. In Kal's closet, a large section had been dedicated to her clothes and shoes, and in the bathroom the second sink and vanity were peppered with all her toiletries. A couple boxes of miscellaneous things, like a few books and picture frames, were in a box on the kitchen counter for her to place where she liked. She'd hoped to kill some time tonight getting settled in, but Kal's minions had taken care of everything already.

"Would you like to see the new nursery?" he asked as they wandered around the house that was now supposed to be her home.

Lana couldn't help the expression of surprise on her face. "What do you mean?"

"It's all done. The store delivered everything this morning, and I paid the interior decorator that did the house to come over and get it all ready to go." Kal took her hand and led her to the room that had until recently housed all his exercise equipment.

A plush moon hung on the door with the name "Akela" embroidered in golden thread. Kal had a wide, excited grin on his face as he opened the door, as if it were Christmas morning. His enthusiasm was contagious and Lana couldn't help smiling, too, as they went inside.

There, she stopped, frozen in place. It was...amazing. The last time she'd been in this room it was wall-to-wall weights and cardio equipment. A massive mirror had stretched along one whole side. It was all gone now. The walls were painted a soft gray to highlight the new wainscoting that wrapped around the room. The gray crib was against the back wall with the moon-and-stars bedding. The mobile that hung overhead had little plush stars in white and blue, and matching decals were sprinkled across the walls like constellations.

There was a coordinating dresser, an armoire and a comfy-looking rocking chair. A crystal chandelier had replaced the previous lighting. Apparently he'd bought far more than she thought while she wasn't paying attention. It was the classiest, most adorable nursery she'd ever seen, fitting in with the rest of the luxurious décor in Kal's house.

Kal stepped inside and opened up the closet. There was the assembled high chair, stroller, car seat and swing. "It's all ready for tomorrow. I'll have to get the car seat anchor installed in the rental tomorrow morning so hopefully we can take Akela home with us right away."

Looking around at everything, Lana felt the emotions start to overwhelm her. The last few days had been so stressful, but Kal had been there for her through everything. He'd gone over and above, by far, and not just by marrying her. Tears started to well in her eyes no matter how hard she fought them.

Kal turned to look at her and his face morphed into panic at her tears. Lana almost never cried. "What's wrong? You don't like it? I thought a gender-neutral set would be best, since I told you I'd donate it all once this was over."

Lana shook her head vehemently. "It's beautiful. I love it." She launched herself into his arms and clung to his chest. He held her tightly and made no moves to pull away. That was one of her favorite things about Kal. She wasn't very touchy-feely, but every now and then, she needed a good hug. He would hold her for as long as she wanted to be held. He never pulled away first.

This time, however, suddenly felt different. He held her the way he always had, but she could hear his heartbeat speed up in his chest. He seemed a little stiff, a little more tense than usual. Memories of their kiss flashed through her mind, drying her tears and making her own pulse quicken. Had their fake marriage managed to ruin their innocent hugs, as well? It didn't feel as innocent as it used to.

Finally Lana straightened up to look him in the eye. She intended to speak but instead found herself in his arms, their lips only inches from each other. They lingered like that, both of them unsure what to do. Lana could feel the current running between them. It urged her to kiss him. At the same time, her rational brain was screaming at her to step back before this sudden attraction ruined their friendship.

That was the thought that snapped her out of it. She took a cleansing breath and smiled. "Thank you for all this, Kal. It's more than I'd ever hoped for. This is all more than I expected. You're amazing."

Kal smiled, a smaller, almost shy smile that made the tiny flecks of gold in his otherwise dark brown eyes twinkle. His square jaw was still a little tense as though he was struggling to hold back all the feelings that had danced between them a moment ago. "You deserve all this and more."

She didn't, but she appreciated that he thought so. "Akela is going to love it," she said, shifting the conversation off herself. Lana pulled away and took a lap through the room, circling the gray-and-white chevron rug and heading back to the door. "You're just too efficient, Kal. I thought I would spend tonight assembling a crib or putting away my things and now I don't have anything to do."

His brow furrowed as he turned to her and followed her out of the nursery. "I didn't want you to have anything to do. I wanted to make this all as easy as possible. What's wrong with that?"

"Nothing," she sighed. She took a hard right to return to the living room and away from the master suite. Nothing aside from the fact that it was their wedding night, and although she knew nothing was supposed to happen between her and Kal, her nerves were getting the best of her nonetheless. Their lingering touches were becoming increasingly potent. "It's just something to occupy my mind."

"Hopefully tomorrow you'll have an infant to occupy you. Tonight you'll just have to cope with the boredom of being married to me."

He smiled wide and Lana felt her belly tighten in response. Their wedding was supposed to be a piece of paper to make the judge happy, but ever since their kiss this afternoon, things had felt different between them. Every touch, every glance her direction stirred a response in her body when it never had before. She wished it would stop. The situation was complicated enough without a sudden attraction to Kal.

Lana turned away and glanced down at her phone. It was just after nine. Too early to turn in but too late to start a movie or something. She really needed a little time away from Kal. That might help the situation. Of course, now they lived together, so there was only so far she could go.

Then she remembered the giant jetted tub he had installed in the master bathroom. It was probably still unused. "I think I'm going to take a bath and break in your new tub," she said. "It's been a long day."

Kal nodded. "There's fresh towels in the linen closet just beside it."

Lana disappeared into the bathroom and, once she shut the door, let her back fall against it to block Kal and all these new feelings outside. She took a deep breath, happy to find the air in here was not scented with his cologne.

She had to shake this off, she told herself as she went to the tub and started filling it. Kal agreed to a marriage on paper, and she wasn't about to repay his kindness by getting all moony-eyed over him now that they were married.

As Lana slipped out of her clothes and pulled a towel from the cabinet, she realized just how odd it was to think of herself as married. It certainly wasn't where she had expected herself to be a week ago. Things had changed so quickly. Then again, it wasn't a real marriage. And this wasn't a real wedding night. And yet her friendship with Kal didn't feel the same as before. Something had changed, something more than just a piece of legally binding paper.

Lana slipped down into the hot, steamy water and felt her muscles instantly relax. She pressed the button on the side, and the jets came to life. They massaged her neck and back, forcing her to enjoy her time there and not worry about everything that was waiting outside the doors.

Eventually, however, the water started to cool and her fingers started pruning. She couldn't hide in the bathroom forever. She had to face Kal again and determine what their sleeping arrangements would be. Although there was a nicely appointed guest room down the hallway, for appearances they probably needed to share the master bedroom. Everyone from the nanny to the cleaning lady needed to believe they were married, but that huge king-size bed didn't seem nearly large enough for the two of them.

Funny how they'd actually shared that same bed before when they stayed up late watching movies and fell asleep, but it hadn't been such a big deal then.

She pulled the drain on the tub and climbed out, wrapping herself in a fluffy white towel. It felt childish, but she avoided leaving the bathroom for as long as possible. She brushed out and braided her hair, went through the complicated nighttime skin care routine she rarely, if ever, did, brushed and flossed, then rearranged all her things on the counter the way she liked them.

When Lana was out of things to do, she scooped up her clothes and carried them with her toward the bedroom. When she stepped out, she found Kal lying on the bed. He had changed into a pair of pajama pants and was propped up with a bunch of pillows, reading.

She tried not to pay too much attention to the carved muscles of his bare chest or how handsome he looked with his reading glasses on. Instead she pivoted on her heel and marched straight to the closet without making eye contact. There, she tossed her clothes into the hamper and searched through her new space for pajamas of her own.

Ones with full coverage, if she had some.

Kal had a really large closet, but not so large that Lana could get lost in it. True, she had to find out where all her things were stored, but after ten minutes, he started to wonder if she would ever come out.

He could tell that things had changed between them. The minute their lips had touched, it was like a switch had been flipped in their relationship. Despite all their agreements going into this marriage about it being on paper, a part of him wondered if that was even possible. Seeing her in that amazing wedding dress, feeling her surrender to his kiss, noticing how skittish she seemed around him…the attraction wasn't in his imagination.

That kiss had unleashed something that the two of them had worked hard to keep suppressed. He was sure they both had their reasons for ignoring the sexual tension that buzzed between them, but now it was nearly impossible. It was exactly what Kal had been afraid of. Pandora's box was open and there was no way to shove the temptation back inside.

That was probably why Lana was in the closet layering on every piece of clothing she had. Not that it would help. He knew each curve of her body—it was on display three nights a week at the luau. They'd hung out by the pool together. His best friend…wife now… had few secrets from him, physical or otherwise.

He was about to investigate her disappearance when the door opened and she finally stepped out. She was wearing less than he expected—a pair of flannel shorts and a relatively skimpy tank top. The top clung to her curves and left little to the imagination without a bra on beneath it. Lana hovered awkwardly by the closet door, so Kal turned his attention back to his book.

"Find everything okay?" he asked.

"Yes." Lana strode to the bed and pulled back the comforter. She crawled in beside him and tugged the sheets up under her arms. On the nightstand was her iPad, and she picked it up to start playing her game of choice.

"Feel free to move anything around in there if you don't like how they put things away."

"It was fine. I just had trouble trying to decide what I wanted to wear to bed."

Kal put the bookmark between the pages and set his book in his lap before he turned to look at her. "Don't change what you would normally wear on my account. I want you to be comfortable here. I know none of this is normal, but this is your home now, too, for as long as this goes on."

Lana looked at him with a curiously raised brow. "I appreciate that, I really do, but I don't think my normal attire is appropriate."

Kal frowned. "Why?"

"I sleep in the nude."

He was pretty sure he'd never blushed in his whole life, but suddenly he could feel his cheeks start to burn. He should've anticipated that answer. He slept in boxers on the hotter evenings and flannel pants on cooler nights. Lana had lived alone for as long as he'd known her, so why wouldn't she sleep naked?

"W-well…" he stammered, "I say do what you want to. We're both mature adults. If you're more comfortable that way, I'm sure we can deal with it."

Lana twisted her lips into a thoughtful expression. "So if I just stripped all my clothes off right now, you'd be okay with that?"

Kal swallowed hard, grateful for the thick comforter over his lap. "Absolutely."

"And that wouldn't make you uncomfortable?"

He sighed. "You're my best friend, and now you're legally my wife. I think me seeing you naked shouldn't be that big a deal. I'm not going to lose all my self-control and ravish you or anything."

Lana's almond-shaped brown eyes narrowed at him. "Okay. If you really feel that way." She reached for the hem of her tank top to pull it up over her head.

Kal froze, his breath catching in his throat. He knew he should look away, but he couldn't even move enough to do that. Was she really going to just pull her clothes off? She'd been more nervous since their ceremony than he was. It seemed like an awfully bold move on her part.

Lana stopped and flopped back against the pillows in a fit of laughter. "Oh my goodness. You should see your face," she managed to get out between giggles. She flushed bright red and her eyes teared up with amusement. "Abject panic."

She was just messing with him. That wasn't nice of her at all. Kal grabbed a nearby pillow and smacked her in the face with it. It silenced the laughter at last as she looked at him, stunned by the assault. "You're evil," he said.

"Oh yeah?" Lana grabbed a pillow of her own and swung it at him. The movement knocked the book off his lap, and the bookmark fell out onto the floor, losing his place.

Great.

Now it was war. Flinging back the blanket, Kal climbed to his knees and grabbed the pillow tight in his hands. He started wailing on Lana in between taking blows to the head and shoulders from her assault. They battled for several minutes until he managed to knock the pillow from her hands. That was when he moved in for the kill. Lana was extremely ticklish and he was going to get back at her.

He lunged forward and his fingers found her sensitive sides and belly.

"Oh no!" she wailed through laughter and tears. "No tickling!" Lana shrieked, but he wasn't letting up.

She scrambled to try and crawl off the bed, but Kal took advantage of her distraction. He climbed over her legs and pinned her arms down to the bed. "Gotcha!" he shouted triumphantly.

Lana struggled beneath his grip for a moment before she realized she'd lost the battle. Her breathing was labored from the wrestling and the laughter, and her normally golden tan skin was flushed and blotchy red from exertion. It was then that he noticed her breasts as they moved up and down against the thin cotton of her tank top. Her nipples were hard and pressing through. She might as well be naked, really, for all the shirt left to the imagination.

He swallowed hard and tore his gaze away to look her in the eye before she caught him checking her out. The light of amusement was gone as she watched him, and something different was in its place. The same something he'd seen after they shared their first kiss this afternoon—a perplexing mix of attraction, confusion and apprehension.

This playful game had suddenly taken a turn into dangerous territory.

For the first time in his life, Kal wasn't sure what to do. If it were any other woman in his bed looking at him that way, he'd kiss the living daylights out of her, then strip off those clothes and make love to her all night.

But this was Lana. His *wife*, Lana. It made more sense and no sense all at once.

He wanted to kiss her again. That kiss earlier had been sweet and unexpectedly enticing, leaving him wanting more. It was his wedding night. A kiss from his new wife wouldn't be too forward, would it?

Before he could decide, Lana's hand reached up, and she threaded her fingers through the hair at the nape of his neck. She tugged his mouth to hers and they collided with the impact of an atom bomb. She made the move, so he put his reservations aside and went with it.

It was nothing like their earlier kiss. This one was fueled by pent-up desire, a taboo attraction and an overwhelming sense of exhaustion that made it impossible to fight anymore. The kiss was hard and Lana's mouth was demanding. He freed her other arm and she tugged him closer to her. Whatever hesitation she might have been feeling earlier had flown out the window, and she was ready and willing to take what she wanted from him.

He almost couldn't breathe from the intensity of their kiss, but he refused to back away from it. When her tongue glided along his lips and demanded entry, he gave in with a groan of need he couldn't suppress. He drank her in, meeting her toe-to-toe with every move.

Kal couldn't remember the last time he'd been kissed with so much passion. Perhaps he never had. He'd suspected that his best friend was a bit of a firecracker in her relationships, but it wasn't something he'd allowed much thought. Now, as her long, shaped nails dragged across his bare shoulders and her breasts pressed urgently against his chest, that was all he could think about.

Every nerve lit up in his body like a neon sign. This was no slow-burning fire; it was an inferno that swept him up. He was hard and throbbing with need after only a kiss. Kal could feel his self-control slipping away with each flick of her tongue across his.

If he didn't take a step back, right now, they would consummate this marriage. Lana had been very clear that it was not her intention going into their wedding. It was supposed to be on paper only. They were on the verge of breaking that arrangement after only a few hours together.

He finally ripped his mouth away and moved back out of her reach. They both lay still and panting for a few moments as they tried to process what had just happened between them.

"I'm sorry," Lana said after a few minutes. She sat up and covered her flushed face with her hands. "I don't know what got into me just now."

"Don't be sorry," he said. "I wasn't exactly fighting you off." Even as he pulled away, he felt his desire for Lana drawing him back in. They needed some space apart. "I think that maybe tonight, I should sleep in the guest room." Kal backed off the bed and picked his book up from the floor.

"Kal, no. You don't have to do that. This was all my fault just now. I shouldn't have…" Her voice trailed off and she shook her head. "I'll sleep in the guest room," she offered. "I'm not going to drive you out of your own bed. That's silly."

He held out his arm to stop her and took another step toward the door. "It's your bed now too, Lana. Stay. I insist. I think I'm going to be up for a while anyway. I'm going to read for a few hours."

Lana's face was lined with conflicting emotions. She didn't want him to go, but they both knew it was probably for the best. There were too many emotions flying around after the day they'd had and what just happened between them was evidence of it all combusting at once. Tomorrow they needed to focus on meeting with the judge and getting guardianship of Akela. That required a good night's sleep. At least for Lana. Kal doubted he would get that no matter where he slept tonight, but being apart would be better for now.

She didn't argue with him. He turned off the lamp by his bedside and backed away toward the bedroom door.

"Good night, Mrs. Bishop."

Five

Judge Kona eyed Lana and Kal as they stood together in front of the bench. She clutched Kal's hand with all her might to keep from shaking. Her nerves were getting the best of her, even with Kal's reassuring touch to steady her. It didn't help that the judge was a very large and intimidating man with a bald head and heavy, dark eyebrows. His eyes were nearly black and seemed to look right through her.

"Mr. Lyon, your attorney, has filed your motion for temporary guardianship of Akela Hale. It looks as though he has everything in order." The judge's sharp gaze dropped to the paperwork as he flipped through everything Dexter had submitted for them.

"I do have a few questions for you. It says here that you are the owner of the Mau Loa Maui Hotel, Mr. Bishop. Is that correct?"

"Yes, sir."

"You and Mrs. Bishop live on the premises?"

"Yes, sir. I recently completed the construction of our home, which is on the property, but on the far side away from the hotel. It's over three thousand square feet with a decorated nursery ready to bring Akela home."

Judge Kona nodded and looked at the paperwork again. "Mrs. Bishop, you are employed at the hotel as a choreographer. Will you be continuing to work?"

Lana took a deep breath and hoped her answer was the right one. "Yes, sir, I will. However, it is a flexible position. We are interviewing caregivers to watch Akela in the home while we are both working instead of putting her in day care."

The judge made a note. "Very good. Now, my understanding is that you two are newlyweds. Bringing a child into the situation will seriously cramp your honeymoon phase. Have you taken that into consideration before making this decision?"

"We have, Your Honor," Kal answered. "We welcome the opportunity to make Akela part of our lives for as long as may be required."

"Mrs. Bishop," Judge Kona said, the name still sounding foreign to her ears, "your sister agreed to a plea bargain yesterday. In exchange for her testimony against Mr. Keawe and his distributor, she is receiving a reduced sentence of two years' probation and mandatory in-house drug and alcohol dependency treatment. If she completes the twenty-eight-day program successfully, she will be released and I will grant her custody of her daughter again. That means you will be her guardian for a minimum of that time.

"If, however, she leaves the program, fails a mandatory drug test or otherwise breaks her probation requirements, she will go to jail for no less than a year. Are you and Mr. Bishop willing to take on your niece in the event that this arrangement is longer than planned?"

"Absolutely, Your Honor." Lana meant it. Kal might not be thrilled with his whole life being uprooted for a year or more, but she was willing to do whatever was necessary for Akela.

Judge Kona's dark gaze raked over the two of them one last time before he sorted through the paperwork and signed off on one of the pages. "Very well. Mr. and Mrs. Bishop, you hereby receive the temporary guardianship of your niece, Akela Hale. Social services will be making several unannounced visits to the home to ensure the child's welfare and safety, in addition to making calls to your provided references. You may meet with the clerk to pick up Akela."

The sound of the gavel smacking the wooden desk echoed through the courtroom and Lana took her first deep breath in half an hour. In relief, she turned and wrapped her arms around Kal's neck. "Thank you for this."

"You're welcome. I knew everything would work out. Now let's go get her."

Dexter escorted them out of the courtroom and they followed him down the hallway to the clerk's office. She thought they might have to go pick Akela up wherever her foster family was living, but she found an older dark-haired woman sitting on a bench in the hallway holding her infant niece.

"Akela!" she shouted, pulling away from Kal to run down the tile corridor to her niece.

The baby was oblivious of what was happening around her, but the woman holding her looked up as Lana came closer and smiled. She stood, shifting the baby on her hip and swinging a diaper bag on her shoulder. "You must be her aunt," she said.

Lana nodded. "Yes." She ached to hold her niece but didn't want to tear her out of the woman's arms. From the looks of Akela, the foster mother had taken excellent care of her. Her blue-and-white dress was clean and well fitting, her dark baby curls were combed and she wore a little white headband with a bow. The baby smiled when she saw Lana, her slobbery grin exposing her first bottom tooth.

"I'm Jenny. I've been watching this little ray of sunshine the past few days. She's very lucky to have family willing to jump through the hoops to take her in."

Dexter and Kal finally came up behind them. "Everything went as planned," her lawyer said. "We've just got to sign some paperwork in the clerk's office and you'll be able to take Akela home."

The woman handed Lana the baby. "Your attorney has my number if you need to get in contact with me. I've only had Akela a few days, but I've cared for dozens of foster children over the years. If you have any questions about babies, feel free to call me. She's been napping about two in the afternoon. This one is teething, and it makes her a bit crabby, so good luck with that."

Lana cuddled her niece into her arms. She'd been worried about who had Akela, but the kind, soft-spoken woman put her fears to rest. "I may take you up on that," she admitted. "I honestly know very little about babies, but that's how most moms start out, right?"

Jenny smiled brightly and patted her arm. "Absolutely. You'll do just fine." She placed the diaper bag over Lana's shoulder. "Everything she had with her when social services picked her up is in that bag. There's a bottle made up for her in the side pocket if she gets hungry before you get home."

"Thank you, Mrs. Paynter," Dexter said before opening the clerk's door and ushering Lana, Akela and Kal inside. There were discussions and forms and paperwork, but Lana couldn't really focus on what was going on. Let her lawyer and her husband handle things. All she could think about was the baby in her arms. It hadn't been the simplest process to get to this point, but it was worth it all.

"How are you, baby girl?" she cooed in the voice she reserved for babies and animals.

Akela got excited by the question, grinning and reaching up with her chubby baby fingers to grab a fistful of Lana's hair.

"Oh, ow," Lana said, extracting her hair and brushing the rest of it over her other shoulder. Lesson one— keep the hair away if you want it to remain in your scalp.

The men's voices got louder and Lana knew they were wrapping things up. Lana gave a gummy kiss to Akela's cheek until she squealed in delight and everyone's attention in the room turned to them.

"Well, okay, then," Kal said with a smile. "I think that means it's time to go home. What do you say, Miss Akela?"

They all headed out to the parking lot together. They'd ridden over that morning in the new Lexus SUV he'd rented while they had the baby. Kal opened the door to the backseat, where they'd mounted the car seat.

"Here you go," Lana said, handing the baby over to him.

There was a momentary flash of panic in his eyes as he held Akela and eyed the car seat with suspicion. "O-kay," he said, quickly recovering. "Baby goes here," he muttered aloud. "Snap this thing. Arm through there. Snap that thing. And then..." He looked around. "Done!"

Lana let her gaze flicker over it for just a moment to ensure that he did it right, but it looked good to her. She didn't exactly know how everything was supposed to be, either. She was the youngest child. Kal was the oldest, but just by a couple years. She doubted he did much to take care of Mano when he was an infant.

They climbed into the front seat and started the car. "Well, we did it," Kal said. "In just a few days, we managed to get married, move in together and gain guardianship of a baby." He ran his fingers though his hair and sighed. "Now what?"

That was a good question. To be honest, Lana hadn't entirely thought the plan through to the conclusion. All she knew was that she needed her niece to be with her. Now that that was accomplished... "Now I guess we just start living like every other family in America."

Kal shook his head and pulled the SUV out of the parking lot. "I hope you know what that means, because I sure don't. Do we need to stop at the store? What do six-month-olds eat? I ordered some formula at the baby store. Does she eat baby food yet?"

Lana bit at her lip. "I don't know." She picked up the diaper bag and started sorting through the contents.

She found a box of something called rice cereal, but it
didn't look like any kind of cereal she'd ever seen before. There were also a couple of small jars with pu-
reed fruits and vegetables. "There's some baby food in
here. Enough to last us today and tomorrow until we
figure out what she likes."

Now that the worry of getting guardianship was out
of the way, Lana found herself blindsided by the fear
that she had no clue what she was doing. "You didn't
happen to buy a baby book at the store, did you?"

"No." Kal turned to her with a wry smile. "You
mean they don't come with instruction manuals?"

"I sincerely doubt that. Thank goodness for the internet." She was Googling everything she could think
of the moment they got in the car.

"Well, I don't know much about babies, but I do
know one thing," Kal said with a laugh. "We need to
interview a nanny as soon as possible."

Day one went better than Kal had expected. Lana
hovered nervously over the baby between feedings and
frantic readings on the internet. Kal, regrettably, had
to leave her to put in a few hours at the hotel, but when
he came home, the house wasn't on fire, the baby was
alive and Lana wasn't drinking hard liquor, so it was
a success in his book.

He played on the floor with Akela for about an hour
while Lana passed out on the couch, and then he and
the baby did a test-run bath with the fancy baby bath-
tub he'd bought. He'd never seen anything like it before—it weighed the baby, reported the temperature
of the water and had a nice place to lay the baby down
where she couldn't slip and slide around. Akela had a

great time splashing around in the water. He wasn't sure how clean she actually got, but it had to be worth something to at least sit in soapy water for a while.

When he was done, he wrapped her in a towel, put on a clean diaper, then slipped her into some footie pajamas they'd bought at the store with little sheep on them. He put her into the baby swing in the kitchen with one of the bottles made up in the fridge and ordered dinner from room service to be couriered over for him and Lana. He might not be in the hotel, but he owned it and got what he wanted.

When Akela finally fell asleep that night, Lana was right behind her. Kal grabbed his phone and took it into his office. He knew he needed to call his brother, Mano, and it couldn't be put off any longer. Some of the hotel staff in Maui worked with the Oahu staff, and if word got back to Mano that Kal had married and had a baby girl, things would get blown way out of proportion.

He was content to keep things quiet for now. He'd only listed his brother as a reference, so Mano was the only one who needed to know about the marriage. They'd successfully gotten custody, and if all went well, in a month Akela could return home and he and Lana could quietly divorce. If things stretched on... well, eventually he'd have to tell the rest of his family. Kal would cross that bridge when he got there, however.

Closing his office door, he dialed up his brother and settled into the leather executive chair he'd chosen for the new house. He leaned back and propped his feet up on the corner of the desk. From there, he had a clear view out onto the lanai. The sun had long set on the golf course, but he could see the lights of the resort in the distance and a sailboat on the water with lights up the mast.

"Hello?" his brother answered with a husky, sleepy voice.

"Aloha, Mano. Did I wake you? It's just past eight."

Mano chuckled and cleared his throat. "You know me, living the wild life. Paige and I fell asleep on the couch watching a movie."

"Watching a movie?" Mano was completely blind and had been for a decade.

"Yes, well, she was watching it. I was just listening. Apparently it was boring even if you can see, and we nodded off. To what do we owe a phone call on this random Wednesday evening? I've barely heard from you since Tūtū Ani's birthday party."

Kal snorted into the phone. "You're turning into an old woman, Mano. Complaining I don't call enough. Next you'll be telling me I'm too thin and I need to eat, like Aunt Kini always does."

"That's what domesticity does to you," Mano said. "Paige and I spent all weekend house-hunting. We have an ultrasound next week where we find out if we're having a boy or a girl. All that focus on home and family makes you look at things differently."

Kal certainly understood, although his brother didn't know that yet. "How is Paige doing?" His brother's fiancée was almost halfway through her pregnancy. She'd just moved from her home in San Diego to Oahu. Kal had yet to go to Oahu and meet her, and he felt bad about that. Work had just gotten in the way, like it did with everything else. Now that he had a wife and child to worry about, he imagined it would get even harder to fit in time for things like that.

What a strange thought to cross his mind so easily... a wife and child. The idea didn't bother him as much as he thought it would. Of course, it was a fake marriage and someone else's baby, but still, the words slipped into his vocabulary easier than he expected after years of resisting the idea of it.

"She's good. I think the move and all the excitement has worn her out. Her ankles swell up at night, so I've been rubbing them for her and ordering milk shakes from room service. She's adequately spoiled."

"What are you going to do when you get a house and there is no room service?"

"Takeout and delivery," Mano answered without hesitation. "I do think we've found a house she likes, though. We're going to put an offer in on it in the morning. It had amazing views."

"How would you know?" Kal and Mano had always tried to make light of his brother's disability. He never wanted him to wallow in it, so their humor was dark where that was concerned.

"It was in the listing, so it has to be true. Besides, Paige made a squealy, girlie sound when we walked out onto the deck. I figure it's nice. The price tag definitely falls in the category of nice view, beach accessible."

"Well, let me know what happens. I'll fly over to see it."

"Sounds good." Mano hesitated on the line for a minute. "So what's the call about? You rarely dial me up just to chat, big brother."

Mano was right. They didn't spend a lot of time

catching up on the minutiae of each other's lives. "I'm calling because I have some pretty big news."

"Well, considering this is my brother, Kalani, on the phone, I'll exclude romantic engagements from the list of options. Have you impregnated your tennis instructor?"

Kal bit his lip. This news really would blow Mano out of the water. It was very unlike Kal. He hadn't so much as mentioned a woman he was dating to his brother by name in years, much less talked about one like there was future potential with them. Mano knew how he felt about commitment. And knowing he'd married Lana of all people... "I gave up tennis two years ago. And my tutor was a man."

"You're growing out your beard," Mano guessed.

"How is that big news?"

"You've never had a beard. I don't know. Just tell me. I'm no good at the guessing games."

"Okay, fine," Kal relented. "I'll tell you, but for now I need you to keep this between us. I don't need the whole family going crazy over it."

"Hmm..." Mano said thoughtfully. "This is going to be good. I promise not to share it with anyone but Paige."

"I said not to share it with anyone," Kal pointed out.

Mano sighed. "When you're a couple, telling me is like telling her by default. If Paige can't know, just don't tell me. I'm physically incapable of not telling her. She won't spill the story to anyone, I promise. So lay it on me."

"All right. I've gotten married." He spat the words out as fast as he could. "And we have a six-month-old little girl staying with us for a while."

There was a long silence as Mano processed his words. Kal waited for the questions, the confused exclamations, but there was nothing. "You always have to one-up me on everything," Mano complained at last. "I get engaged, you get married. We're expecting a baby, you come up with one already born. You can't let me have anything, can you?"

"I'm not kidding, Mano. Lana and I got married yesterday. We got guardianship of her niece today."

"You and *Lana*?" His voice went up an octave in surprise. Mano had met Lana once when he came to the grand opening of the Maui resort. He knew they were close friends, but married? Even Kal couldn't believe that. "Wow. I mean, you told me she was an amazing person and crazy gorgeous, but I thought you two were just friends."

So did he. Then they got married. And then they kissed and he questioned everything he'd believed about their friendship. "She is amazing and gorgeous and a great friend. It's a long story."

"You also swore up and down that you'd never marry."

Kal's jaw tightened. It was true. And it still was true in terms of a real marriage and family. But he couldn't say that. "I realized that I wanted more and so did she. She changed my mind about the whole thing. We decided to just take the plunge before one of us chickened out."

As much as Kal wanted to tell his brother the truth, he couldn't risk anyone finding out the marriage was a sham. If they lost custody of Akela for lying to the judge, he'd never forgive himself, and neither would Lana. Everyone had to believe the story for it to work.

"And how does the baby come into play?"

"It belongs to her sister. I'd already proposed when we found out that she's in rehab and the father is in jail for selling drugs to a cop. We went ahead and got married sooner than later so we could take the baby."

"Wow. Married with a baby…a sister-in-law in rehab… There's a lot going on over on Maui."

Kal chuckled. "You have no idea. It's a ton of information to process, I know, but I wanted to tell you so you heard it from me and not the staff."

"Thanks for that. You know how they love to spread gossip. I feel like I should say congratulations, and yet I'm not certain. As a man recently in love, I find I don't hear that edge of panic in your voice that's usually associated with love and marriage. Are you sure you're excited about these sudden developments? You've asked me not to tell anyone, which seems weird for a joyous event. No one has blackmailed you into doing this, right?"

Not exactly. A little arm twisting perhaps, but he'd given in easily for Lana. "I married Lana of my own free will, I just don't want the family swarming yet. It was a lovely ceremony."

"That's good to know. I never imagined you getting married, but now that you have, I'm glad it was because you wanted to. I have to say I'm a little disappointed to miss out on the major event. It's less than an hour's flight, you know. Paige and I could've come. Or are we part of the pesky swarm you're avoiding?"

Kal tried to ignore the slight sound of hurt in his brother's voice. They teased each other so much it was hard to tell if he was messing with him or seriously regretted missing the wedding. "Of course not. It was just the two of us. Not a big deal. You didn't miss anything. I'm sure your wedding extravaganza will far outshine ours."

Mano made a grumbling sound under his breath. "I have no doubt of it. Paige keeps meeting with Tūtū Ani, plotting and planning. We want to get it done before she has the baby, but I can feel the ceremony and the budget growing exponentially every time they get together."

"Got a date in mind?"

"Valentine's Day, I think. Probably at the new house. The yard was big enough."

Kal needed to note that on his calendar. It was a busy time in Hawaii, with everyone desperate for a romantic getaway somewhere that wasn't covered in snow and ice. He wondered how he'd explain to his brother when he showed up without a wife or a baby. Or how would he explain it to everyone else if he did? This relationship had an unstable timeline, and that made it hard for him to plan. It wasn't forever. It was fake. But how long would they fake it? He had no idea.

If Mele screwed up and Lana got the child for months, even years, would she expect them to continue this marriage? He wasn't sure, but it certainly would complicate things. Considering they were two days into their marriage, he opted not to worry too much about it.

"Let me let you go," Kal said at last. He didn't really want Mano pushing for too many details. As soon as Paige got wind of the news, Kal was sure Mano's fiancée would start asking questions neither Mano nor Kal could really answer.

"Enjoy the honeymoon phase," Mano said with a snicker.

"You bet I will," Kal said, trying to sound like an excited new groom. He wasn't sure he pulled it off. As Mano said, he was missing that edge of panic. "Aloha," he added, hanging up.

Now that was done, he had to face another uncomfortable situation—climbing into bed with his wife again.

Six

Lana noticed when Kal finally came to bed that night after eleven, but she was too tired to care. That baby had worn her out completely. She rolled onto her side away from him and snuggled into the blankets, falling back asleep before his head likely hit the pillow.

It seemed like only minutes later that she rolled onto her back and found herself in bed alone. This time, sun was streaming in through the windows. It was morning. She looked at the clock by the bed. It was just after eight. She didn't expect Akela to let her sleep this late.

She sat up and picked up the baby monitor to make sure it was working. It was turned off. The nursery was far enough away that she might not hear the baby crying if she'd accidentally forgotten to turn it on or the battery died. In a panic, she flung back the blankets and moved quickly across the wooden floors of the hallway to the nursery. To her surprise the door was open and there was no baby, crying or otherwise, in the crib.

Then she heard the distant sound of baby giggles. Lana followed it back down the hallway and through the living room to the kitchen. There, she found Akela in Kal's arms and Kal shirtless in those blasted pajama pants again. This time, putting together a bottle for the baby with one hand.

"Good morning," she said, rubbing the sleep from her eyes.

"Good morning," Kal replied. He held up the bottle to her. "It turns out that baby cereal isn't really cereal. I mean, it is. When they're older you can feed it to them with a spoon, but since we aren't sure if she's been eating a lot of solids yet, you can add some to the formula and it gets a little thicker and more satisfying. Who knew?"

Lana crossed her arms over her chest and eyed Kal with suspicion. "And who told you that?"

"My grandmother."

Her eyes widened in surprise. "You told your grandmother about Akela? Did you tell her we were married, too?"

"No." Kal tightened the nipple and gave the bottle to Akela. She reached up for it and helped him hold it to her mouth. "I told her that I was helping you babysit for your sister. There was some in the diaper bag the foster mother gave us, so she said this was the best way to start her off if we aren't sure. She said we could also try some smooth baby foods and even Cheerios to see how she does."

Lana just nodded blankly as he spoke and was wondering if she had actually woken up or if this was all some weird dream. It didn't feel like a dream. And yet the events of the past week had culminated in a moment that didn't seem real. This moment felt so domestic, so unlike the life she was used to living. She was married, living in a home with Kal and they were caring for a baby. It was everything and nothing she'd wanted all at once. All she could do was stand dumbstruck in the kitchen while he fed Akela.

After their first awkward night together in the house, they hadn't had a moment like this. They'd quickly gotten it together in the morning and gone straight to court. Now everything was settled into a domestic bliss that she didn't entirely mind. It was certainly better than living alone in that hotel suite. But she wouldn't let herself become too comfortable. All of this was temporary. The minute she started liking the idea of being married to Kal and having this little family, it would all fall apart. She couldn't get wrapped up in the fantasy they'd crafted for Judge Kona.

"Would you like some coffee? I just brewed a pot."

"Sure." Lana found a mug in the cabinet and poured herself a mug of black coffee. Normally she put cream in it, but she needed a straight shot of caffeine to face another day of motherhood without any help. She wasn't sure how people did it. Generation after generation had managed, so she could, too, but working at the same time would make things complicated.

Kal leaned back against the countertop and watched the baby happily suck down her formula. "So, I called the employment agency today to ask about getting a nanny."

Perfect. It was as though he'd read her mind. "When can they send someone over?" She hated to sound anxious, but she'd missed a lot of work. Given she hadn't taken a sick day in all the years she'd worked at the Mau Loa, she hated missing performances now.

"They're sending over a couple candidates for us to interview tomorrow."

"Tomorrow? That means they probably won't start until the next day at the earliest. I've got a show tonight and rehearsals the next day. We were working on a new *South Pacific* routine before all this came up. Are you going to watch Akela while I work?"

"I could. Or we could get someone to watch her tonight. But I don't think it's a big deal for you to stay home with her if you want to. It might be the best thing to help her adjust to a new situation."

"Kal, I missed the show on Tuesday as it is. I can't miss another night."

"I know your boss," he said with a sly grin. "He's not going to fire you."

"Very funny."

"Okay," he relented. "I'll get someone to watch her this evening during the show, okay? I'm sure I can get a volunteer on staff who would much rather babysit than clean hotel rooms or bus tables."

She felt better. A little. She didn't know why it was bothering her so much. She was the one who insisted on getting custody of Akela. Did she think she could put the baby in the cabinet when she was too busy to deal with her? Kal had signed up to marry her, not to take on caring for an infant. He was already going above and beyond for her.

"Thank you." She reached out her arms. "Here, give her to me. I know you need to get in the shower."

Kal nodded and handed the baby over to her. "I'll

text you when I get someone pinned down for tonight. What time do you need to leave to get ready?"

"No later than six-thirty."

Kal turned to head toward the master suite when the doorbell rang. He frowned and looked at her. "Are you expecting anyone?"

Lana shook her head. "No one I know realizes I'm living here."

He went to the door and looked through the peep hole before shrugging and opening the door. "Hello. Can I help you?"

When it opened all the way, Lana could see a petite woman in a frumpy black suit standing on the doorstep. "Hello, I'm Darlene Andrews with Honolulu Child Services. I'm here to conduct a random review of Akela's home environment."

They hadn't waited long. Kal took a step back to allow her inside. "Please come in, Ms. Andrews. I was just about to get in the shower."

"Please, go ahead," the woman insisted. She pointed to Lana where she was standing with Akela in her arms. "I can speak with Mrs. Bishop while you're getting ready."

Kal looked at her, obviously not wanting to leave Lana alone with the woman, but she shrugged him away. The bigger deal they made out of this, the stranger it would look. "Go on, honey. I don't want you to be late to work."

He reluctantly disappeared and Lana turned to the woman with a smile. "Would you like some coffee? Kal just brewed a pot."

"Yes, thank you."

She followed Lana into the kitchen, where Lana

made her a mug and placed it on the counter. "Is there anything specific you need to see while you're here?"

"Since this is our first visit, I'd like to do a quick walk-through of the house, especially the nursery, to make sure you have adequate facilities for the baby. Then just a few short questions and I'll be out of your way."

"Okay. Follow me and I'll show you Akela's room." They wandered through the living room and down the hallway to the nursery. Lana opened the door and stepped inside so Ms. Andrews could get a good look at it. There was no way she wouldn't be impressed with the room. It was the prettiest nursery in the history of nurseries.

Ms. Andrews didn't react, however. Instead she made notes and checked off items on some form attached to her clipboard. She examined the crib closely and then the stroller and car seat combination that was near the closet. "Very good. And where do you and Mr. Bishop sleep?"

Lana pasted on a smile. "We're on the opposite end of the hallway, here." She checked the bedroom before she pushed the door all the way open, and the bathroom door was shut. She could hear the shower running. "You'll have to excuse the mess, we just got up."

Ms. Andrews paid particular attention to the unmade bed and the two places where Lana and Kal had obviously slept together the night before. She never imagined they would pay that much attention, but she was thankful she hadn't taken to sleeping in the guest room. Then again, maybe Ms. Andrews was looking at the baby monitor and Lana was just paranoid. She couldn't be sure.

When they returned to the living room, they took a seat opposite each other on the sofa. "How are you and Mr. Bishop adjusting to caring for a baby?"

"The last day has been a steep learning curve for both of us, but I think it's going well so far. Kal has a large family on Oahu and they've been just a phone call away for support and questions."

Ms. Andrews nodded and made a note. "My file says that you told the judge you were planning on hiring a caretaker for Akela while you work?"

"Yes. We have interviews scheduled for tomorrow. I'm hopeful we'll find just the right person to take care of her."

"Will she be a live-in or part-time nanny?"

Lana had no idea. "She will be full-time, but as for whether she moves in with us, I guess that depends. I have some late hours at work, so if Kal can be home, it's not an issue. Having someone around the clock would certainly be a help, but I think that will be something we have to discuss with the nanny we end up hiring. We do have a guest suite if we need it."

The woman seemed to take notes for what felt like an eternity. Lana hoped she said and did all the right things, but she couldn't be sure. She kissed Akela on the top of her head, drawing in her sweet baby scent, and tried not to worry about it.

Finally the social worker looked up and smiled. "I think for now that's all I need. Akela seems to be doing well so far and you've set up a nice home for her with the two of you. If I didn't know better, I'd think she was yours." Ms. Andrews organized her paperwork and slid it back into her leather briefcase bag. She stood and shook Lana's hand. "Thank you for your time."

Lana walked her to the door and stood there holding Akela as she stepped out into the morning sunlight.
"You'll be hearing from me again," she said with a polite, detached smile.

Lana returned the smile and stepped back inside.
She was certain they would.

Tonight was the first night that Kal had watched
Lana perform in the luau as his wife. Less than a week
ago, he'd stood in the exact same spot and done the
exact same thing, but everything was different now.

Before, when Lana had danced sensually onstage,
he'd tried hard not to notice. She was his best friend
and employee, so the shimmy of her hips and the hard
muscles of her exposed core weren't his to admire. But
now they were. Sort of.

The pulsating sound of the drums as she moved
her body made a bolt of liquid heat surge through his
veins. Each flash of thigh from between the large ti
leaves of her skirt made him wish it crept just the tiniest bit higher. He wanted to run his hands over the
smooth skin of her inner thigh and press a kiss against
the belly that was exposed to the crowd.

Just the image in his mind of doing that made every
muscle in his body tense up. He was overwhelmed with
need, driven by it for the first time in his adult life. He
felt like an overstimulated teenage boy, aching almost
to the point of pain to reach out and touch her. He had
managed to keep his hands to himself the last couple
nights, but he couldn't imagine sleeping beside her
again without reaching out to her.

Life and dealing with Akela had distracted him from
wanting Lana, but now that things were settling down,

he couldn't shake these thoughts. The sight of her in her wedding gown with the plunging neckline, the memory of that red-hot kiss on their bed…it haunted him every time he had a free moment to himself. And now, seeing her dance, he was on the verge of losing his tight grip of control.

This was what he'd been afraid of with Lana. What he'd fought so hard to avoid. She was everything he'd ever wanted but knew he couldn't have. Marriage had never been his forte, but a temporary one wasn't so bad. Going into it knowing it would end, without any false expectations of forever, made it much more tolerable. The hardest part so far was not enjoying the benefits. That was their agreement—a sensible one at the time—but now he regretted going along with it. If he was going to have Lana for his wife on paper, he wanted her for his wife in bed, as well.

When her last number finished, Lana met him in the back of the courtyard. She'd changed backstage this time into a short, strapless dress in a bright tropical pattern. That didn't help matters. It clung to her curves and showcased the legs he'd been admiring earlier.

"Are you ready to go? We need to relieve the babysitter."

Lana nodded. "Once we get the nanny position filled, I'll be more comfortable staying all the way to the end and giving notes. Tonight I've got Pam watching for feedback to give them at rehearsal tomorrow. So far, the audience really seems to enjoy the new singing number at the end."

Aware of the people around them and desperate for an excuse to touch her, he reached out and grabbed her hand. "Let's go home, then."

She didn't resist taking his hand and following him to the lot where he parked the Jaguar. Once they arrived home, Kal paid the young woman from housekeeping for watching Akela, and she left quickly.

Akela was asleep. They poked their heads into the nursery to check on her, but all was well. She was in her sheep jammies and contentedly dreaming in her crib. So far, Akela had slept through the night, which was nice. And after that show, he hoped the trend continued tonight.

"I'm exhausted," Lana said as they shut the nursery door and headed toward the master bedroom. "I thought being a dancer was hard work, but being a dancer and having an infant to care for is masochism at its finest."

"Well, if it makes you feel better, you're a beautiful masochist."

Lana dismissed his compliment and stepped out of her sandals. Reaching behind herself, she strained to reach the zipper of the dress.

"Here," Kal said as he tugged off his tie. "Let me get it."

Coming up behind her, he grazed her skin with his fingertips as he reached for the clasp. Lana lifted her hair up, exposing her bare neck and shoulders, and sending a whiff of Plumeria to his nose. His skin tingled as it brushed hers, undoing the clasp and running the zipper down to the small of her back.

When he reached the bottom, the rough lace of her panties peeked out at him, and he could feel the desire he'd suppressed surge through him again. Kal didn't let go the way he should then. Instead he moved closer, until his warm breath brushed over her bare shoulders.

Lana didn't move away, either. She stood very still, drawing in a ragged breath and slowly letting it out. Kal rested his palms on her shoulders, relishing the silky feel of her skin under his hands. He wanted to touch more of her and prayed that she'd let him.

She leaned back against him, finally swooping her hair over one shoulder. As she lowered her arms, Kal felt the fabric of her dress slip away until it pooled at her feet. His gaze ran over her shoulders, finding no strapless bra where he expected it to be. Of course not...they didn't wear anything like that beneath their traditional outfits. It complicated costume changes backstage.

One glance at her full, mocha-tipped breasts was enough to undo him. "Lana..." he said in a pained voice as his fingertips pressed into her shoulders. The single word expressed everything he needed to say to her in that moment. That he wanted her. That he knew he shouldn't. That one more minute together like this and he wouldn't be able to tear himself away.

Lana didn't respond. Instead she reached up for his hands and moved them around her until they cupped her breasts. His own groan muffled her soft sigh of pleasure as the weight of them rested in his hands. He brushed his thumbs over her nipples and they hardened to peaks that pressed insistently into him.

Leaning down, Kal pressed his lips against her shoulder. Her skin was warm against his lips and smelled like cocoa butter and tropical flowers. He traveled up the exposed line of her neck, inhaling her scent into his lungs. He teased at the sensitive hollow beneath her ear, biting gently at her earlobe until she gasped.

"Kal," she whispered, and arched her back to press

her rear into the straining length of his erection. The movement elicited a growl from deep in his throat, a sound he didn't even know he was capable of making until then. Lana was able to rouse something from deep inside him. Something primal that he'd never let out before.

He got the feeling that if he truly let go with Lana, there would be no going back. He didn't just want to make love to her, he wanted to claim her as his own. Kal had no right to do that. She didn't belong to him. But that was what she drew out of him. "Last time I pulled back, Lana. I pulled away when I didn't want to because I thought we'd both regret it. And yet we're here again. I don't think I can walk away from you twice."

Lana turned in his arms to face him. She looked at him with her dark, almond-shaped eyes and there was no hesitation there. No concern. Nothing but a blazing desire for him that he'd never seen from her before. Perhaps something new and primitive had been released in her, as well. "Then don't."

If Lana felt the slightest hesitation about making love to Kal, it was only in that moment when he finally gave in to wanting her and she saw the passion unleash in him. He was a large man, a strong man, but although she wasn't afraid of him, she wondered in that moment if she was enough woman to satisfy the lust that rolled off him in waves.

Then he kissed her and her doubts were put to rest. His powerfully possessive kiss and firm desire against her belly proved that he wanted her and only her. His fingers dove into her hair, pulling her close and refus-

ing to let her go. All she could do was cling to him and
go along for the ride. This was something she'd always
wanted but had been too afraid to have. Now was her
chance and she needed to make the most of every second in case this never happened again.

His tongue invaded her, deepening the kiss and demanding more, which she gladly gave. Then, just as
suddenly, he pulled away, ripping his lips from hers.

Lana thought for a moment that he had gathered
his senses and was about to walk out, but he just stood
there. His breath was ragged and his gaze never left
her body as he tugged off his tie and slipped out of his
suit coat. She was standing there in nothing but the
nude panties they wore under their dance costumes.
Lana had never felt more exposed yet more desired in
her whole life.

Feeling bolstered by his attraction to her, she hooked
her thumbs under her panties and slowly slid them over
her hips. Kal watched with his mouth agape and his
shirt half unbuttoned as she shimmied them down her
legs and kicked them to the side. Then, completely
naked, she planted her hands on her hips and waited
for him with a sly smile curling her lips.

The rest of his clothing came off much faster, and
suddenly she was hit by a wall of hard, male flesh. It
pushed her back until she fell onto the mattress. Kal
covered her body with his own, hardly allowing her
the opportunity to enjoy the view as he had. Instead
his mouth was on hers again and his hands were roam-
ing over her exposed flesh.

Lana loved the feel of his weight pressing her against
the mattress and the insistent desire against her thigh.
She parted her legs, letting Kal nestle between them

just as he started moving lower down her body. His lips nibbled and tasted at her throat, her collarbone, her sternum, and then finally he drew one nipple into his mouth. He sucked hard, teasing at her sensitive flesh before soothing it with his tongue. The power-ful caress sent a bolt of sensation straight to her core. Her insides grew molten as they began to pulse with the insistent rhythm of need.

As if he could sense her building demand for his touch, Kal reached between her thighs. He brushed over her ever so faintly once, then twice, making her nearly want to scream with pent-up desire, even though she knew she couldn't risk waking the baby. Then his fingertips delved deeper, finding her sensitive cen-ter and drawing a silent cry from her throat. Lana couldn't keep her hips from moving against his hand. She needed Kal's touch. She needed Kal.

She wasn't sure how much longer she could wait. Lana appreciated the extended seduction that Kal likely had planned, but she was ready to jump to the main course. "Do you have..." she gasped between strokes "...protection?"

Instead of answering right away, he slipped a finger inside her, making her whole body tense up and a soft whimper pass her lips.

"I do," he answered as he slowly, torturously, moved in and out of her. "Are you sure you want me to go get it so soon? I was just starting to have some fun."

Lana bit her lip as he continued to tease her, ver-bally and otherwise. Her muscles were tightening with building sparks of pleasure that she wasn't ready to give into yet. "Get it," she managed between clenched teeth. "Now."

Kal grinned wide and pulled his hand away. "Yes, ma'am." He moved to the side of the bed and returned a moment later with a condom in his hand. She took advantage of the view, spying the hard length she'd been longing for. Her eyes widened for a moment as she watched him sheathe himself in latex. Kal was above average in all ways. This would be interesting.

As quickly as he'd left, Kal returned to his place between her thighs. Instead of entering her, he continued to tease at her with his hand. Whether she wanted to or not, she was responding to his touch. He was driving her toward the edge before they'd even begun.

"Not yet," she gasped, reaching one arm out to caress the stubble on his cheek. "With you."

His dark gaze met hers, and then he nodded silently. His body hovered over her on his powerful arms. She drew her knees up, opening to Kal when she felt the press of his desire. "Please," she urged, and finally felt him move into her.

It was slow, but Lana closed her eyes and enjoyed every moment of it. She bit at her lip again to hold in a gasp of pleasure as he sank deeper and deeper. Kal moved one hand to clutch her hip and lift her up to take him all the way. When he was finally buried deep inside her, they both let out a soft groan of pleasure.

Kal dropped onto his left elbow and pressed a softer kiss to her lips. Then he started rocking in and out of her. All the sensations he'd aroused in her earlier returned at once as he retreated, then advanced more forcefully each time. The ratchet inside her moved one notch higher with every thrust. Her soft cries and gasps were a steady chorus in the tropical evening air.

Then Kal let go of her hip and slid his hand down

her leg to the back of her knee. He sat up, hooking her leg over his shoulder, and planted a kiss on the inside of her knee. Looking into her eyes, he thrust again, deepening his reach tenfold. Lana couldn't hold on much longer. She clawed at the sheets as he pounded deep inside her, until at last she couldn't resist it and shattered into an explosive orgasm. Her whole body shuddered with the power of it. She grasped a pillow and used it to smother her cries, gasping Kal's name into the fabric as he continued the pleasurable assault on her body.

He wasn't far behind. Gripping her leg in one hand and her breast in the other, he thrust one last time and came undone with a silent roar. He shook with the force of his release, as though it were sucking out every ounce of energy he had; then he pulled away and collapsed onto the bed beside her.

Lana lay there for what seemed like hours with her mind racing, although it was only minutes that passed. She couldn't quite believe what had just happened. Instead of enjoying the moment and basking in the afterglow, she anxiously awaited Kal's reaction. She didn't regret it, but once the erection faded and reality set in, would he?

She was beginning to think he'd already fallen asleep when he rolled toward her. He wrapped one large, protective arm over her waist and tugged her body against his. Curled against him, she found it harder to worry. With his warm breath on her neck, she snuggled into the pillows and gave in to sleep.

Seven

Things in Kal's world were finally getting back to normal. At least, back to normal in terms of work. He'd returned to the office and Lana was in the dance studio with her team and performing in the luaus with them again. Nanny Sonia had started. She was the fifth nanny they interviewed and came highly recommended. Akela was instantly drawn to the older woman and the choice was easy to make.

So far, she was amazing, working happily with their strange hours. Even though they hadn't originally asked for a live-in caretaker, that was where they'd ended up. Once Kal and Lana were working again at all hours, it was just easier for Sonia to move into the guest room. It was next door to the nursery and had an en suite bathroom so she had plenty of her own space.

At home, things weren't *quite* the same. At least not

since the night they'd given in to their desire for each other. Looking back, he couldn't quite figure out how it happened, but he refused to regret it even though he knew he should. It was a night he'd never forget. How could he? His best friend—the one with the fist bumps and reluctant hugs—had given herself to him in a way he'd never imagined possible. Or maybe he had, which was why he'd kept his distance.

The last thing done for the night, Kal decided to head home. Normally he would put in a few more hours walking the resort and making sure the guests were all happy. Lately he'd just rather go. Even with the situation being different, he found that he looked forward to the end of his day more than he had when he was a bachelor. There was actually someone waiting for him at home. A houseful of someones.

It hadn't taken him long, but he found he missed those chubby cheeks and that toothless grin while he was at the office. That must be why people always put pictures of their family on their desk. He'd never understood that before, but he was considering it now. He found he was also missing Lana. They'd spent more time together than ever before, but it wasn't enough. The more he had with her, it seemed like the more he wanted. It was a dangerously slippery slope, but a part of him was tempted to see where it would lead.

That night, when he walked in the front door of the house, he wasn't sure what he expected to find, but what he got was a hell of a lot more.

Christmas had arrived in Maui.

In the great room, a huge Christmas tree was placed in front of the picture window. It was decked out in a rainbow of ornaments, lights and tinsel. A silver star shone on the top. Between the tree and the pine garland that went across the fireplace mantel, the house was thick with the fresh scent of real, imported Norfolk pine from the mainland.

Four stockings hung beneath the pine garland, one for each of them, including Nanny Sonia. The coffee table had a festive poinsettia runner and bowls of sparkling ornaments and peppermint candies. There were lights and candles all around the room, and festive Christmas music playing in the background.

Kal wasn't entirely sure what to say. He didn't own any Christmas decorations. This was his first Christmas in the house and he hadn't given much thought to the holidays with everything else going on. It was such a busy month at the resort he was more concerned with decorating the hotel and pleasing his guests than worrying about his own place. Who would see it aside from him anyway?

"You're home!" Lana said as she came out of the kitchen and spied him, dumbstruck by the front door.

"I am. Is this our house?" he asked. "It looks a little like our house, but not really. Now it looks more like the North Pole than Hawaii."

Lana beamed at his words. "It does, doesn't it?"

"Where did all this come from?"

"The store. I just realized that this was going to be Akela's first Christmas and I wanted it to be nice. It's also our first Christmas together, so I thought people might think it odd if we didn't decorate at least a little bit. I had some free time this afternoon, so I went crazy at the home store."

"It looks great," Kal said. He listened and heard Akela babbling in the kitchen over the crooning sounds of Bing Crosby on the wireless surround-sound system. "What are you all doing in there?"

"We're baking cookies." Lana reached for his hand and pulled him into the kitchen.

Akela was sitting in her high chair with a bottle of juice and a scattering of Cheerios. Sonia was pulling a tray of just-baked cookies out of the oven.

"Are those chocolate chip?" Kal asked, his mouth starting to water involuntarily as the smell hit him.

"Yes," Sonia said brightly. "It's my grandmother's recipe. We've also baked white chocolate macadamia nut cookies, sugar cookies, coconut snowballs and fudge."

"Wow," Kal said. He reached over and snatched a cooling cookie from one of the wire racks and shoved it in his mouth. It tasted like gooey, melting chocolate butter heaven, if that was even a thing, and it should be. "I love cookies."

The holidays had always been a big deal with his family, but like most things, they were more traditionally Hawaiian than mainland Christmas. There was always kalua pork in the imu, lomi salmon, coconut haupia for dessert, and Santa or *Kanakaloka*, wearing flip-flops and his best Hawaiian shirt.

He did get a taste for more Americanized Christmas from his father, however. His father was born and raised in upstate New York before he joined the navy and ended up stationed in Hawaii. While his father was happy to fall in love with a Hawaiian girl and escape the hellish New York winters once and for all, there were things he still missed. He would go shopping at the PX for things he couldn't normally get here, like gingerbread cookies and peppermint candy canes.

More of it had made its way into stores over the last twenty years, but when Kal was a kid, those special treats had been his favorites. Especially the cookies.

Lana looked at him with a frown. "I never knew you liked cookies."

"Who doesn't like cookies?" he replied, snatching another off the rack.

"Well, I mean, I didn't know you were so fond of them. You've never been big on desserts when we've gone out."

"That's because most restaurants don't offer cookies. Especially warm ones." He reached out for a third, but Lana smacked his hand.

"Pace yourself."

Sonia giggled and continued to scoop another batch of dough onto the cookie sheet.

Lana looked down at her watch. "You know what, Sonia, you were supposed to go off duty half an hour ago. Tonight is your weekday evening off."

Once they decided that Sonia would be a live-in nanny, they arranged for her to have all day Saturday and Wednesday nights off. There weren't luaus on either day, so Lana or Kal could be home with Akela when she was gone.

Sonia turned to the kitchen clock in surprise and dusted her hands off on her apron. "You're right! I have book club tonight. I'd better get cleaned up and get out of here or I'll be late. Do you mind if I take some of the fudge for the ladies?"

"Not at all."

Sonia quickly made up a small plate of fudge squares and hurried to her room to get ready to leave.

Once they were alone, Kal and Lana worked together to clean up the last of the baking stuff and put the cookies and candies in airtight containers.

"Those cookies are great, but I think I need more than that to eat tonight."

"You're right. It's about time for Akela's dinner, too. If you can feed her one of those jars of baby food, I'll see what I can find in the pantry to make for our dinner."

Kal looked at her with unmasked surprise. "You're going to cook?"

Lana crossed her arms over her chest in irritation. He couldn't help noticing the way she cocked her hip and pressed her breasts tight against her shirt with the movement. Even though he'd seen Lana perform in a lot less clothing, this was better. He liked seeing the casual side of her—her womanly curves evident, but hidden away like a treasure he ached to seek out and uncover again. Most of the time at work, she was in performance mode or strict choreographer mode. Neither was much fun to be around, frankly.

"Watch it, mister." Lana smirked and turned her back on him to look in the refrigerator.

He'd be lying to himself if he said he didn't also like her in sassy wife mode. In their home, with her hair up in a messy bun and a clean, fresh face. In their bed, with her cheeks flushed and her eyes glassy with desire. As she bent over to look in the fridge, the clinging yoga pants she wore after finishing dance rehearsal that morning highlighted one of her best assets. Those hips were carved by Mother Nature to be cupped by his palms. He could still feel the silk of her skin against his, making his hands tingle with the memory of touching her.

Things between them had been a little awkward since they had sex. They'd both tried to dance around the issue and deal with everything *but* that. It was easy to ignore the tension and ignore each other when the baby needed to be fed and work beckoned. He didn't want it to be that way. He didn't know how long this situation would last, but he wanted the best of both worlds—the mind-blowing sex and the amazing friendship they'd had before. It made sense that they should enjoy the physical pleasures…they were married, weren't they? It shouldn't cost them the easygoing friendship he enjoyed. He didn't understand why one had to affect the other.

Maybe tonight, after Akela went down for the night and Sonia was out for the evening, they could talk about it. That was one thing they hadn't really had the opportunity to do since it happened.

And maybe, if he was lucky, she'd let him make love to her again.

Lana had to admit that having Sonia around made a world of difference. She felt better being back at work and didn't pass out with exhaustion the minute her head hit the pillow. Akela was another matter. Sonia kept that baby busy. They went on walks, played peekaboo, read books and had plenty of tummy time. After a bath and a quick change into her pajamas, now it was the baby who was out cold when she laid her out on the crib mattress.

"Was she fussy?" Kal asked as she came back into the living room.

"Not at all. She's already asleep. Between Sonia and the lavender bubble bath, she doesn't stand a chance."

Kal nodded and looked at her with the same dark eyes she'd fallen prey to the other night. "Come sit with me."

Lana was considering cleaning up after dinner, but it didn't take much to convince her to put that off. Kal was sitting on the sofa near the gas fireplace. It was rare that you needed one in Hawaii, but with the Christmas lights twinkling and the candles around the room flickering, it added a bit of ambience.

Kal had changed out of his work suit. He was in a pair of jeans and an old surfing T-shirt she'd never seen before. The way it clung to his broad shoulders and large arms, he probably had bought the thing in high school. It looked good on him, though. He was handsome as always in his power suits, but when Kal had jeans on, it meant it was time for fun, not time for work. That was the time she enjoyed the most.

Lana settled onto the couch beside him and accepted the glass of wine he offered. "The house looks beautiful," he said. "I mean it. I spent a fortune having an interior decorator put this place together, and in a single day you made it feel more like a home than it ever has."

She swallowed her sip of wine, surprised by his words. "Thank you. I'm glad you like it. It's just a few things. I didn't want to take over your whole house, but I wanted to make a good Christmas for Akela's first."

"It's your house, too, Lana. If you want to decorate the whole place, I'll give you my credit card and you can go crazy. This is a special occasion."

Lana tried to shrug that off. They both knew this wasn't a real marriage. Sex hadn't changed that any more than their vows had. "I'd hold off on buying a

commemorative ornament, since we won't make it to
our second Christmas."

Kal sighed. "Other people don't know that, though."
He stretched and wrapped an arm around her shoulder.
"At the very least you have to admit that this is quite a
romantic setup with the lights and the fire."

"It is." She hadn't thought of it that way at the time
she put it all up, but she hadn't envisioned snuggling
on the couch with him like this, either.

"It's a shame you didn't hang any mistletoe."

Lana stiffened. Apparently they needed to have the
discussion they'd avoided since they had sex. If Kal
was under the impression that it was going to happen
again, he was wrong. She'd let herself get wrapped up
in the moment, falling under the spell of the fantasy
they'd crafted for appearances, but she couldn't let it
continue. She knew her heart and how easily she could
fall for Kal. That would only end in heartbreak for her.

He would walk away from this whole thing like it
was just another adventure they'd shared without carrying any feelings for her. He might want her physically while they were together, but he didn't want to
be with her beyond this arrangement. Lana knew that.
Sex just led to thoughts of a future they wouldn't have.
She couldn't do that to herself. "I don't think mistletoe
is the best idea, Kal."

"Sometimes the worst ideas are the most fun, Lana."

She turned to pull away from the arm that was
cradling her to his side. "Kal…that night between us
was…"

"Amazing?"

"A mistake," she corrected. "I think we both let
this fake relationship get the best of us, but it can't

continue. It just clouds our friendship with all these physical complications."

"Physical complications? What's an orgasm or two between friends?"

Lana ignored his smirk. "I'm serious, Kal. You might be the master of sex without strings, but we've got a lot of history together. I don't want things to get complicated. Our friendship is so important to me. I don't want to compromise it."

Kal's face grew uncharacteristically serious as he reached out and caressed her cheek. "The last thing on this earth I'll do is hurt you, Lana. If you're not attracted to me—"

"I didn't say that," she interrupted.

"Then you *are* attracted to me," he said with a mischievous twinkle returning to his eye.

Lana sighed. This conversation was not going the way she'd expected it to. Was Kal truly attracted to her? She couldn't imagine it. "The point is not if we're into each other."

"I think that is the point, Lana. Listen, I know that we're not compatible in the long run. We want different things out of life and relationships. But this is a special opportunity we've been given to enjoy our time together. We're married. We might as well enjoy some of the perks. I think it will carry over out of the bedroom and make our relationship seem more authentic in the eyes of others."

"And when it's over?" Lana asked. Were they just supposed to go back to the way things were before? Was that even possible?

"And when it's over, it's over. You go back to hunting for your soul mate and I regain my crown as the most eligible bachelor on Maui."

Lana shook her head. She knew she couldn't just go back to looking for another guy the way she had done before. Being with Kal might have very well ruined her for every other man. But right now she was more worried about how the two of them moved forward together. "So our friendship just goes back to the way it was before all this? I don't see how that's possible."

Kal sighed and sat forward in his seat, pinning her with his dark gaze. "Lana, the minute you proposed to me, our friendship changed. It will never be exactly the way it was. When we married, when we kissed, when we had sex…all those things changed it. But that's okay. Relationships aren't meant to be static. They evolve. We might as well enjoy where our friendship is right now while it lasts, because it will evolve to something else in the future. It's not better or worse, it's just the way life is.

"And no," he continued, "I'm not offering you that white-picket-fence future you want when this charade is all over. It's what you want and it's what you deserve. One day you'll find it, but you and I both know it won't be with me. You know me better than anyone else, so you know exactly what I'm offering and what I'm not. So why can't we enjoy where our friendship has evolved to right now? Indulge in the physical while it lasts?"

Kal very nearly had her convinced. It all sounded good in theory. Keeping her emotions out of the situation would be hard, but maybe she could do it. He was right—her eyes were wide-open where he was concerned.

"Lana, you can't tell me that in all our years of friendship, you hadn't been the tiniest bit curious about what it would be like to make love to me. I'll be honest and say I thought about it. A lot."

"Kal!" Lana complained.

"We're being honest here," he insisted. "Tell me that you never once fantasized about me."

Lana tried not to squirm under his heated gaze. Of course she'd fantasized about him. She wasn't about to admit to how much, though. "I can't. You know full well I can't say that."

"Okay, then tell me you didn't enjoy the other night."

This time Lana frowned. "You know I can't say that, either." It was incredibly evident she'd had a good time. If she hadn't worried about waking the baby, she would've screamed the house down.

"Okay, then." His hand reached out to stoke her bare arm. The caress sent a shudder through her whole body that would've betrayed any lie she told about not wanting him. "So let's just stop stressing out about the whole thing and just do what feels right for us. If that means making love every night…" He let the words hang in the air between them. "…then so be it."

That was certainly a tempting offer. The idea of spending the upcoming weeks getting to know every inch of Kal's hard body was a benefit of this arrangement that she'd never anticipated. It might not be smart but was definitely tempting. "You're working pretty hard to convince me to sleep with you again, Kal."

A smile curled his lips. "Harder than I normally have to work, I assure you."

"Good. You should have to work for it. All those women falling all over you just inflates your ego."

"You're always there to take me back down a notch. It's a bit of a turn-on, I have to say. Most things about you turn me on." Kal looked at her with desire hooding his eyes as he spoke. She never imagined he'd look at her that way and yet here he was, talking about her as if she were some kind of sex siren. "What do you say we retire to the bedroom for the evening and I help you get on Santa's naughty list?"

Lana leaned in close, considering his offer. If he really did like it when she was sassy, she'd be sure he got a good dose of it. "Hmm..." she said thoughtfully as she ran her hand over the stubble of his cheek and down the tight fabric of his T-shirt to his bulging biceps. "That sounds like a nice offer, but I've got a better one."

"What's that?" he said with eager interest.

"I cooked dinner, so you need to clean the kitchen. That's how marriage works. And when you're done, then maybe," she said seductively, letting her thumb brush over his bottom lip, "I'll let you earn some coal for your stocking."

Kal wrapped his arms around her waist and tugged her into his lap. "How about we earn the coal and then I clean the kitchen? Does the order really matter as long as it all gets done?"

Lana considered his counter offer with a smile. "I suppose not."

In one swift movement, Kal stood up from the couch with Lana in his arms and started carrying her toward the master bedroom. She bit back a yelp of surprise, hoping not to wake the baby. She clung to his neck and buried her face in his soft, worn surfing T-shirt as they went down the hallway. The scent of him permeated the fabric, and once she drew him into her lungs, her whole nervous system seemed to spring to life.

She was instantly ready for him. As much as she had resisted this mentally, her body was on board with getting as much of Kal as she possibly could before all of this was over. Her nipples were tight against her top and her breasts ached for him to touch them. She felt her core turn to warm liquid when he looked down at her and smiled. One time together was all it had taken to train Lana's body. This time she was ready without so much as a kiss.

Kal sat her at the edge of the bed, and she wasted no time pulling off her top. They both quietly and swiftly cast aside their clothes. He pulled away long enough to shut and lock the bedroom door in case Nanny Sonia came home early, and then he crawled onto the bed beside her.

He immediately drew her body against his, and her upper thigh made contact with the firm length of his need. Kal groaned aloud, and then caught himself. He sat still, not even breathing for a moment, to see if he'd awoken Akela. When he realized it was still safe, he pressed his lips to hers, smothering any more sounds.

They came together quickly in a tangle of legs and blankets. Lana gasped silently as he filled her. She clung to him even as he rolled onto his back and brought her with him. She flipped onto her knees, bracing herself with her hands as she found herself astride him. Kal pulled her down against his chest until her face was buried in his neck, and then he started moving slowly beneath her.

It was an agonizing journey to release, with each moment slow and deliberate. They moved silently together in the dim moonlight of the bedroom, the quiet gasps and heavy breathing sounding like a cacophony in each other's ears. Their bodies tensed and flexed together, Lana sensing he was getting close by the rapid beat of his heart and the press of his fingers into her hips.

When her release came, she buried her face in his throat and nearly sobbed as the waves of pleasure rocked through her. Kal bit tentatively into the thick muscle of her shoulder as he held her still and fought to hold himself back, but he was lost. The flutter of her orgasm coaxed one from him, and he poured into her, his mouth agape with unexpressed feelings.

Lana rolled off Kal onto her side of the bed and took a deep breath to recover. Even their quick, frantic lovemaking was amazing.

She was on the verge of closing her eyes and drifting off to sleep when she felt Kal's weight shift on the bed. When she looked up, he had stood and was tugging his clothes back on.

"Where are you going?" she asked.

"A deal is a deal," he insisted. "I'm going to clean the kitchen. And when I'm done, I'm coming back in here with that container of chocolate chip cookies."

Lana wrinkled her nose. "What are you going to do with a whole container?" He was going to make himself sick eating all of them.

"I don't know yet," Kal admitted. "But even if all I do is line your beautiful, naked body with them, lick melted chocolate from your nipples and eat them off you one at a time, it will be the greatest meal I've ever had."

Eight

You need to come home. Now.

Kal frowned at his cell phone and the disconcerting text he'd just gotten from Lana. Is Akela okay? Did social services come back already?

Everyone is fine. But you're going to want to come home and see who's showed up. Note: it's not social services this time.

He was usually in the office for another hour or so, but he knew better than to ignore this message from Lana. He slipped his phone into his pocket and walked out of his office. "I'm heading home," he said to his assistant, Jane, outside the door. "I don't think I'll be back. Something came up."

Jane looked at him with concern lining her face.

He may have stopped staying late, but he still wasn't the type who left in the middle of the day. "Is everything okay, sir?"

"I think so. Just unannounced visitors from the sound of it. Call the night manager on his cell phone if something happens before he arrives."

He slipped out and got into his convertible. It only took a few minutes to drive around the property to his house, but the suspense was killing him. When he arrived, there weren't many clues, either. Only nanny Sonia's car and the rental SUV were parked out front. Whoever had arrived must have come by taxi.

It wasn't until he walked in the door that he realized who had invaded. It all made sense now. His brother had flown over from Oahu.

Mano was sitting on the couch with his Seeing Eye dog, Hōkū, at his side. A thin, yet pregnant woman with long brown hair was holding Akela on her lap and cooing at her. Nanny Sonia stood out of the way as though she didn't want to intrude on the family gathering but didn't want to be thought neglectful of her charge, either. And then there was Lana, who turned to look at him with an expression of pure panic lighting her dark eyes.

"Honey," she said in an overly sweet voice she never ever used when she spoke to him. "Look who's here to spend Christmas with us."

Christmas was three days away. They weren't just visiting. They were unannounced holiday houseguests.

Everyone turned and looked in Kal's direction except his brother, who had on his dark Ray-Ban sunglasses. His attention was focused on the woman beside him, who Kal assumed was Mano's fiancée, Paige.

He tried not to look dismayed by their arrival, pasting an excited smile on his face. He ensured that he matched the tone with his voice so Mano couldn't call him out for it.

"Wow. I didn't know you two were coming here for the holidays. This is such a great surprise. If you'd told me, I would've reserved our best suite for you at the hotel."

Everyone stood up to greet him. Mano made his way over with Hōkū at his side. He hugged his brother and took a step back. "You almost sold me on that," he said, speaking low. "And of course I didn't tell you. I want to be here at your new home, getting to know your bride and niece, not tucked away in that boring old hotel."

The smirk on Kal's face said everything. That phone call announcing his sudden marriage had sent up warning flags that even his busy brother couldn't ignore. Mano was using Christmas as an excuse to come down here and spy on him. Sneaky little weasel.

Well, two could play at that game. "Mano, you've met Lana before, haven't you?"

Mano turned expectantly and Lana quickly stepped forward to take his hand. "It's good to see you again, Mano."

He laughed and pulled her in for a hug. "There's no handshakes in this family. You'd better get used to that now before you meet the rest of them. Congratulations to you and Kal. He didn't let on that you two were serious."

Kal ignored his brother's pointed tone. "Well, you of all people know how quickly love can strike. In two weeks' time, you and Paige went from strangers to lovers to an engaged couple. Are you going to introduce us to the lovely lady whom I presume is your new fiancée?"

"Of course. Everyone, this is Paige Edwards."

Paige handed the baby back to Sonia and stepped forward, smiling uncomfortably at the strangers who were now her family. Kal didn't know what he was expecting of the woman who captured his brother's heart, but it wasn't what he'd gotten. She was tall and thin, pale and nervous-looking. But there was a light in her eyes that Kal immediately recognized as love and affection for his brother, and that was enough for him. He was excited to learn more about her and find out what had drawn the two of them together while she was vacationing in Hawaii.

"It's nice to finally meet Mano's brother, and now, his sister-in-law!" she said. "He talks so much about you."

"Does he, now?"

Mano placed a hand on his fiancée's rounding belly. "And this, we found out for certain yesterday, is our daughter, Eleu Aolani Bishop."

There was another round of cheers and congratulations. Kal was pleased they'd chosen their mother's name for the baby's middle name. She would love that. "There's so much to celebrate," Kal said. "If you'd told me you were coming, I'd have been prepared with champagne and food in the refrigerator." They really didn't have much but some snacks and baby food. Thank goodness he had a second guest room and room service at his fingertips. It wasn't as well appointed as Sonia's room, but it was somewhere for them to sleep with no notice.

"I'm sorry, Kal," Paige said, nudging Mano's shoulder. "I didn't like the idea of dropping in unannounced, but he insisted you two do it all the time."

"All the time, as in never once in all these years," Kal countered with a grin.

"Mano!" Paige chided, and smacked him playfully on the arm. "You tricked me into imposing on your family." Mano just shrugged, refusing to look guilty for what he'd done.

"You're not imposing. Really. The more the merrier at Christmas, right?" Kal looked to Lana for support.

"Absolutely. I was just telling him the other night how excited I was for Akela's first Christmas and our first Christmas as a married couple. It will be so much more memorable with family here to share it with us. This is your first Christmas together, too, right?"

"It is," Paige confirmed with a beaming smile. "We have plenty to celebrate."

"Mano," Kal said, "I'll show you to the guest room and we can carry your bags back there. Ladies, why don't you decide where you'd like to go for dinner tonight? I'll have some food delivered in the meantime so we aren't eating crackers for Christmas Eve."

Mano gripped Hōkū's lead and followed him to where their bags and a stack of unfamiliar gifts were waiting by the door. Kal picked the bags up and started through the house to the spare bedroom. Once they reached it, he set the bags out of the walkway. "The bed is here on the left just when you come into the room. The bathroom is just past the closet on the right."

Mano just nodded passively with Hōkū panting at his side. "Great. Thanks for putting us up on such short notice."

Since they were alone, Kal turned to look at his

brother. "You mean no notice. Are you here just to spy on me?"

"No. I'm not just here to spy on you. I'm here to introduce you to Paige, to meet your new wife and spend the holidays with my brother." He smiled wide. "And to spy on you."

"You haven't told anyone in the family about this, have you?"

"Of course not," Mano said with a frown. "You told me not to. That doesn't mean I'm not going to fly over here and see what the hell is really going on after social services calls me with a lengthy interview to make sure this is all legit."

"And what did you tell them?"

"That you two are madly in love, of course."

Kal narrowed his gaze at his brother, although his annoyed expression drew no reaction, since he couldn't see it. Instead he crouched down to give his brother's service dog—a friendly chocolate-brown Lab—a good scratch behind the ears. "Good, because it's true. You're going to be disappointed, brother. There's nothing scandalous here to find. Just a happy, newly married couple caring for their niece for a few weeks."

Mano stood for a moment, studying his brother's words. He couldn't rely on visual cues, so he was quick to notice tone, word choice and physical response. It made it harder than hell to lie to him, but Kal had gotten better at it over the last ten years. Considering everything going on, Mano was the worst person to crash their fake marriage, but also the only one he'd dare trust with the truth. Hopefully he wouldn't have to spill his guts before the holiday was over.

"Okay, then." Mano seemed satisfied. For now.

Standing back up, Kal said, "Let's go back to the living room and see where the ladies chose to eat tonight."

Mano nodded to him. "Can you believe we both have ladies? Us? The Bishop Bachelors have finally been tamed."

"A great loss to the women of the islands, I must say."

Kal's brother was right. At least where Mano was concerned. Kal wasn't exactly tamed by love, although his wild nights out would cease until he was officially divorced. He might not be in love with Lana for real, but he wasn't about to cheat on her, either. Mano had really tripped and fallen in love, for sure. Kal had never seen or heard his brother as entranced with a woman as he was with Paige. The time they were apart earlier had nearly destroyed Mano. He'd chased Paige all the way to San Diego to propose and ask her to move to Oahu to be with him. That was serious stuff for a man who'd had a sporadic string of affairs over the years but insisted he wouldn't settle down and be a burden on a woman.

Paige didn't seem burdened. She seemed pretty happy. When they came back into the living room and her eyes fell on Mano, her face lit up. Suddenly she was more beautiful than she had been before, and Kal understood more about his brother's love for her. It radiated out of her.

It made Kal wonder, marriage or no, if he'd ever have a woman look at him that way. He'd never wanted that before—it came with a level of commitment he couldn't give—but suddenly he had a longing for it that he'd never expected. Had he made the wrong decision keeping himself emotionally isolated? Mano certainly seemed happier than he had been alone.

"What have we decided for tonight?" Kal asked, trying not to let the thoughts of his parents' death creep in and ruin his mood.

"Well, Paige has never been to Maui," Lana explained, "so I thought we'd go to your rooftop restaurant. It's hard to beat the view or the food."

"Great choice." Unlike Mano, who put a pair of penthouse suites at the top of his resort, Kal had opted for an exclusive restaurant. With wall-to-wall windows, it had a three-hundred-sixty-degree view. To the east, lush green mountains and to the west, the ocean and views of nearby Lanai and Molokai.

"I told her we might even see whales tonight."

Kal nodded. "That's true. This time of year, the humpback whales are just arriving from Alaska. By February, the waters between here and Lanai will have the densest population of humpbacks in the world. It's an amazing sight. Hopefully you'll see at least one while we eat. Why don't you two get settled in and relax, and I'll make a call to the restaurant to hold the best table?"

Paige nodded and joined Mano to head back to their room. Kal noticed the way she clung to him, guiding him gently without dragging him around. He hadn't been sure his brother would ever find a woman who could get through his defenses, but Paige was obviously the love of his life.

Turning to look at Lana and her concerned frown, he wondered if they'd be able to pull off a relationship that convincing over the next few days.

Lana couldn't remember the last time she'd lain on the beach and enjoyed a little sun. It was the kind of indulgent rest and relaxation she rarely allowed herself. Having Kal's brother and Paige visit was the perfect excuse. Tonight she was performing the last luau before Christmas, but she had hours before she had to be ready.

Turning her head to look at Paige, Lana reached for the sunblock. "I think you'd better put more of this on. You don't want to be burned and miserable on Christmas."

Paige sat up on her chaise and accepted the bottle. "My skin just isn't meant for the tropics. I've taken to wearing SPF fifty just to walk from one side of the resort to the other. No major burns yet, though. I wish I had beautiful brown skin like yours."

Lana smiled. "Thank you. I think you have a lovely complexion, though. So creamy and even. I think women always want what they don't have."

"You're right. I've wanted curves all my life and now that I have this baby belly and pregnancy breasts, I'm not so sure. This isn't what I had in mind."

"You'll have a beautiful daughter when it's over. Maybe she'll end up with Mano's coloring."

Paige stiffened and turned to look over her shoulder to where the brothers were playing with Hōkū and Akela in the surf. "I thought Kal would've told you this, but Mano isn't the baby's father. At least not biologically. In every other way, he's convinced the child is his."

Lana perked up in her seat. "Oh. No, he didn't tell me. You're very lucky, then. Mano seems absolutely smitten with you and his baby. I had no idea from the way he talked about his daughter."

Paige nodded. "I am the luckiest woman on the

planet. You must know what that feels like. I can't imagine being so in love that you would just run off one day and elope without telling anyone. That's so romantic, like Romeo and Juliet or something. With a happier ending."

"He's amazing," Lana said. She didn't have to lie to Paige about that, because it was true. Kal was amazing in every way. That was part of the problem of having him for a best friend. No matter how hard she tried, she knew she couldn't find a man like him and wouldn't be able to have him for herself. She wasn't in Kal's league.

There was no sense in letting herself fall for Kal, no matter how he smirked handsomely at her or treated her like a princess. He might be attracted to her, and keen to continue their physical relationship while they were married, but it wouldn't last. He'd said as much. She knew he didn't really want to get married and she wouldn't be the one to change his mind about the convention.

Both women turned back to the brothers. They hadn't opted for swimsuits, but they were both in T-shirts with their pants rolled up to walk barefoot in the water. Kal had Akela in his arms. Occasionally he would dip down and let the cool ocean water tickle her toes until she squealed, and then he'd stand up again and give her kisses on her chubby baby cheeks. Hōkū splashed around happily, his tail wagging so hard his whole rear end wiggled from the force of it.

They were a handsome pair, both brothers tall and lean with thick, dark brown, almost black hair. They both had lazy beards growing in from skipping a day or two of shaving, making them look more alike than ever before. They were a hard duo to resist as they played with a dog and a baby.

Akela had gotten Kal wrapped around her finger in no time. Lana hadn't been so sure how this would go, since he wasn't much of a kid person and never wanted his own, but he was whupped. She noticed that sometimes even when Sonia was around, he'd take the baby and give her a break just to play with her and hear her infectious baby giggle. The big, important hotelier was a huge softie under those expensive suits. All that baby girl had to do was push out her little bottom lip or bat her full, dark eyelashes and Kal was tripping over himself to make her happy. Kind of how he did with Lana.

The difference was that the baby didn't know that she didn't get to keep Kal, and Lana did. She wished she was ignorant enough to enjoy the time with him that way.

"Paige! Lana!" Kal called, and pointed out at the water. "Come quick!"

The women got up and jogged through the sand to where the boys were standing. "What is it?" Paige asked.

"The humpbacks are breaching. Just wait for it."

The two couples gathered on the shore and waited for the whale to make its next appearance. Five seconds later, a great gray mass leaped from the water and came back down with a huge splash.

Paige gasped and clung to Mano's side. "Oh, wow," she whispered. "It's incredible. I wish you could see it," she added softly. There was a sadness in her voice that Lana understood. She wanted the man she loved to enjoy the moment as much as she did. Kal had told her that his brother tried not to dwell too much on losing his vision. People traveled from all over the globe to see the sights that were just out his window, but he was unable to see them. If Mano let himself wallow in those thoughts, he'd probably never get through the day.

"I don't need to see it," he said as he nuzzled her ear with his nose. "I experience it through you, *pelelehua*."

Lana tried not to melt on the spot listening to the two of them. His pet name for her was butterfly. So sweet. To avoid intruding on their moment, she moved to Kal's side and he put his free arm around her shoulder.

"Watch, Akela," he said, as though the infant could follow along with what they were seeing. "See that tail come up out of the ocean? And that little cloud of misty water shoot up? That's the whale breathing."

A few minutes later, one of the whales breached again and Lana felt her chest tighten. She'd seen these whales every season when they returned to Maui to have their calves in the warm waters. It was beautiful and exciting, but she'd never really given it all that much thought, much less stood transfixed on the beach and watched it happen like a tourist.

Somehow it meant more to do it here with Kal and Akela. With her brother-in-law and future sister-in-law. It felt like she was sharing the moment with family, not just her friends. With her family as it was, it was something she'd never really had. As she watched the back of a whale arch up, then slip beneath the waves with a small calf by its side, she felt a similar sinking in her gut.

She was getting too attached to this life they were building just for show. All this time she'd been worried about the sex, but that wasn't the issue. The sex was great. But she also liked having dinner with Kal at the end of the day and listening to him sing old Hawaiian folk songs to Akela while he gave her a bath. She enjoyed waking up to a mug of hot coffee he'd made for her and rolling over in the night to feel the warmth of his body near to hers.

It was like her dream of a family was coming true, and yet it was the simple things that were getting to her. They were the moments that she would miss the most when all this was over. The whole wedding had been her idea, but she was starting to regret it. It was possible that she could've gotten custody of Akela without all this, but now...? How was she supposed to go back to her life the way it was before? Living out of a hotel room, eating out every night and dating one loser after the next held almost no appeal to her now. Not when she compared it to sharing a home with Kal, cooking dinner for both of them and taking time away from her job to have an actual life.

It might not be a *real* life, but it was all she had. And the longer this charade went on, it was all she wanted. Not just a marriage and a family, but *this* marriage and *this* family. She wanted the sweet, tender romance she saw between Mano and Paige. They had come from two different worlds and yet their lives had meshed together so well. Was it possible that she and Kal could have that for themselves?

Lana took a deep breath and dismissed all those thoughts. She'd promised Kal that this would be a simple arrangement for the sole purpose of getting guardianship of her niece. There wasn't supposed to be any kind of entanglements, physical or emotional. Physical entanglements were a problem almost immediately, but she knew she had to hold back when it came to her emotions. Getting attached to Kal was a recipe for heartache.

As she clung to him, Kal leaned in to plant a kiss on Akela's forehead and then one on Lana's lips. He looked down at her with an excited smile and a light in his eyes and Lana knew instantly that it was too late.

She had made the mistake of falling in love with her husband.

Nine

Kal had spent the last three Christmas Eves with Lana. It was their unofficial tradition, although this year would be decidedly different from the previous ones. The twists would be the addition of his family and Akela. The constants would be Lana and sushi. Traditions had to mean something.

He and Mano drove up the coast to pick up the large order of sushi from the same place where he'd celebrated his wedding day with Lana. The big, traditional Hawaiian Christmas meal would be tomorrow, courtesy of the hotel cooks. Lana and Paige had spent part of the morning working on a couple fun desserts that they wouldn't tell the men about. Honestly Kal would be just as happy to find another container of those chocolate chip cookies that he'd missed, but he was curious to see what the ladies would come up with, too.

Paige had more American ideas about the holiday, so maybe there would be a treat he'd never tried before that could rival the cookies.

As they pulled back up at the house, Mano reached for Kal's arm to halt him from getting out of the car. "Hey," he said. "I want to tell you something before we go inside."

Kal killed the engine and sat back in the seat. "Sure. What is it?"

His brother's expression was almost sheepish, a look he almost never—if ever—saw on him. "I wanted to apologize to you. You were right, I came down here just to see what kind of angle you were playing with the marriage bomb you dropped. I thought maybe the whole wedding scheme was just about getting the baby or that maybe Lana was from another country and trying not to get deported or something. I really wasn't sure. But spending the past few days with the two of you has convinced me that I was wrong to doubt you."

Kal stiffened. He needed to stop his brother from apologizing when he was right all along. "Mano—"

"No," Mano insisted. "I need to say it. You two really are amazing together. What's better than marrying your best friend, after all? You're happier than I remember you being since Mom and Dad died. You and Lana seem to really be in love and happy together, and I'm so glad for you."

Kal didn't know what to say. His brother was one of the most perceptive people he knew. He picked up on the little things. He was damn near a human lie detector test. But he was all wrong about him and Lana. That baffled him. Certainly they weren't good enough actors to pull the wool over Mano's eyes, but he truly believed that they were in love. What did his brother sense between them that Kal didn't?

He watched as his brother's expression grew more serious. "You were never the same after our folks died, Kal. It was like you were afraid to let someone get close just to lose her again. I did the same thing, but for different reasons, and now I know it's no way to live your life. You can't let fear rule you. I'm so glad that both of us figured that out before we ended up spending our lives all alone."

Kal couldn't respond to that, because this time it was painfully accurate. His brother had nailed the issue on the head and made him feel foolish for it. "We've got some great things ahead of us," he replied instead.

Mano smiled. "We do. Let's get in there and eat some sushi. That stuff smells amazing. I'm starving."

They went into the house together and laid out platters on the dining room table. There were California rolls, spicy tuna rolls, unagi eel rolls, crunchy tempura and smoked salmon rolls and an assortment of nigari, all artfully arranged by the *itamae*, or head sushi chef, at Sansei. They also had bowls of edamame, fried tofu, a cucumber salad and some teriyaki chicken for Paige.

Looking down at it all, Kal realized he shouldn't order sushi when he was hungry. It was a shame that Nanny Sonia was spending the next two days with her family. The four of them had their work cut out for them.

They gathered at the table with Akela in her high chair. Lana poured warm sake into cups, with a specially requested Sprite for Paige.

"Wow," Paige said as she took in the spread of food

in front of her. "I don't even know what half of this is, but it all looks wonderful. I think sushi for Christmas is a fun tradition, even if I can't eat much of it this year. It's different. I'm excited to try this."

"Do you want to steal it for our own?" Mano asked. "Make it a true Bishop family Christmas Eve tradition?"

"I think so. There's only so much turkey a girl can eat around the holidays."

"Turkey?" Mano frowned at her.

Lana laughed and turned to Paige. "We don't really do turkey for Christmas here," she explained. "It's all about the pork and seafood dishes."

Kal sat back and watched his new family chat while they ate. He'd really begun to like Paige, and the change in his brother was night and day. Lana fit right in, joking and laughing. It was something he never really expected to have, much less to enjoy. He'd always imagined himself and Mano as lone wolves—the Bishop Bachelors. Now there were wives and babies, holidays and gatherings. It was like he imagined things would've been if their parents hadn't died and derailed their lives. They'd almost gotten back on track.

Almost, if his relationship with Lana was more than temporary. Kal presumed he would enjoy time with his brother and Paige even when Lana was no longer his wife, but things would be different. Unbalanced. She would be off living her own life, Akela would be back with her mother, and Kal would be alone again.

For the first time in ten years, Kal balked at the idea of being alone. He was surprised at how quickly he'd gotten used to all this. What did he do with his evenings before he was having dinner with Lana and bathing Akela before bed? He was working all the time. He didn't miss that at all. The hotel was running just fine without him hovering over his staff every moment.

Kal shoved a spicy tuna roll in his mouth and chewed thoughtfully while the others continued to talk and eat. He didn't want to return to being a workaholic. He wasn't sure that the idea of marriage and family really suited him, but *this* marriage and *this* family were perfect in the moment.

That was the problem, he supposed. He liked it too much.

The holidays were drawing them all together in a way he hadn't anticipated, but he'd have to make a bigger effort to keep emotional distance from Lana when they were over. If his brother was picking up on some kind of connection between them, it meant that more was happening than they'd agreed to. That would have to be squashed before it got worse and feelings got hurt. Whether it was his feelings or hers, he wasn't sure.

"So, do we get to open presents tonight or in the morning?" Paige asked after they'd all stuffed themselves.

"We've always exchanged gifts on Christmas Eve," Lana said. "Is that okay with you?"

Paige nodded eagerly. "I don't think I can wait until morning. I'm like a kid when it comes to Christmas."

"Well, let's clean up and I'll get Akela ready for bed," Kal said as he stood up. "Then we can have some of the top-secret dessert you all made today and open a few gifts."

Kal scooped up the baby and took her into the bathroom for her nightly lavender bath. Fed, clean and in a pair of Christmas pajamas Lana had purchased with snowmen on them, he put her down for the night with promises of Santa coming in the morning—not that she really understood, of course.

By the time he returned to the living room, everyone had gathered there. The ladies presented their desserts—a tall red velvet cake with cream cheese icing and homemade peppermint marshmallows dipped in chocolate. Kal opted to put his marshmallow in his coffee, which was heavenly with the cake. He'd never had red velvet before and it was definitely a Christmas indulgence.

Paige went over to the tree first, sorting through the wrapped gifts and picking out a select few for everyone. Kal and Lana had made an emergency run the day after his brother arrived to get gifts for their unexpected guests. They'd shown up with a big bag of wrapped presents even though Kal and Mano rarely exchanged gifts. It had to be Paige's influence on him.

After a few minutes of frantic unwrapping, it was done for the night. Lana had gotten Kal a nice pair of ruby and gold cuff links and a bottle of his favorite scotch. Mano and Paige gave him a set of his favorite action movies on Blu-ray disc, a remote control drone and an ugly Christmas sweater with Santa on it.

Paige squealed so loudly over the emerald and diamond tennis bracelet that Mano bought her that Kal never did find out what she bought him. Eleu's birthstone would be an emerald unless she came early, and each stone in the bracelet was at least a carat. Kal would probably have squealed, too.

When it was all done, Kal turned to where Lana was sitting on the couch, pouting. "What's the matter?" he asked, knowing full well that she was mad he hadn't gotten her anything.

"Nothing," she said, not meeting his gaze.

"Did you think I forgot you?" he asked.

"Maybe. Of course, you've done a lot for me lately, so it's fine."

Kal reached into his back pocket and pulled out a set of car keys. He dangled them in front of her face, giving her a moment to process that they weren't the keys to his Jaguar or the rental Lexus. There was an unmistakable Mercedes logo on it.

Lana frowned at the keys for a moment. Then he watched it all click into place on her face. Her dark brown eyes grew wide; then she looked in panic from him, to the keys and back to him. "Are you messing with me?" she asked.

Kal dropped the keys into her hand. "Why don't you go look in the garage and see?"

Lana leaped up from the couch and dashed through the kitchen and laundry room to the garage door. They normally parked out front, so the garage was reserved for tools and the boat he never took out. But parked in the far bay was a sapphire-blue four-door Mercedes SUV.

"I thought I could return the Lexus to the rental place after Christmas," he said with his hands buried casually in his pockets.

Lana ran to the car, opening the door and sliding inside. The interior smelled of leather and new car, one of the best scents she could imagine. She ran her hands over the steering wheel and caressed the dashboard. "This is really mine?"

"Yes."

"It's not a lease? I don't have to take over payments?"

That would be cruel. "No, it's all yours, free and clear. Now you can drive Akela around in your own car and not get wet when it rains."

She just shook her head in disbelief. Finally she stepped out of the car and looked over Kal's shoulder to the doorway. "Do you two mind watching Akela while I take Kal for a spin?"

Paige grinned. "Not at all. You two have fun. Don't run over any reindeer out there."

Lana's heart was racing a mile a minute as she started the car and opened the garage door. She backed the SUV out of the driveway at a crawl, afraid that somehow she would ruin her new toy almost immediately. She couldn't believe a car this nice could really be hers.

She took her time getting a feel for the Mercedes as they drove around the resort property, and then she turned out onto the highway. They drove south along the western coast of Maui, past Lahaina toward the central part of the island. She finally pulled over at a high overlook where tourists usually stood with cameras and binoculars to watch the humpback whales. No one was out there this late on Christmas Eve, however.

"Do you like it?" Kal asked.

"Do I like it?" Lana repeated as she turned off the car. "Of course I like it. But it's too much, Kal. You've done so much for me lately, I didn't need to get a single thing for Christmas. The wedding, the nursery, the lawyer's fees, the rental car..."

"No more than you deserve."

She shook her head. She didn't feel like she deserved

all this. She felt naughty knowing she had broken the rules of their arrangement and he just didn't know it yet. What would he say when he found out she'd gone and fallen in love with him after he told her not to? Lana didn't need a luxury SUV, she needed a reality check.

Could anyone blame her, though? Whether or not Kal meant to, he was doing everything in his power to make her fall in love with him. She couldn't resist his charms. He'd gone from being her playboy best friend to a thoughtful and caring husband and father. When he was with Akela, her heart swelled with emotions watching them together. He was a skilled and tender lover, and a romantic at heart, even if he didn't know it or admit it to himself.

She was doomed.

Lana wasn't sure how she would ever be able to repay Kal for everything he'd done for her. Somehow the cuff links didn't seem like enough. She wanted to give him more, but she only had a few things to offer— her heart, her body and her soul. She'd gladly give him all three, although she knew he'd rather just have the body part. So she'd give him that, and he just wouldn't know he was getting the whole package.

Putting on the emergency brake, Lana turned to him. "While we're out here alone, I wanted to say thank you." Then she slipped her red cashmere sweater over her head and tossed it in the backseat.

Kal looked around the deserted highway for a moment with concern, then turned back to her. His gaze flickered over her red lace bra and then he licked his lips. "You're very welcome."

Lana tugged her skirt up her thighs, then crawled

over her new console to straddle his lap. The spacious leather seats provided enough room for her to sit there comfortably and wrap her arms around his neck.

Her lips met his without hesitation. She enjoyed kissing him more than almost anything else. He knew just how to kiss her without overwhelming her like some men did. His kisses were erotic and sweet, arousing her and bringing every possible nerve ending to attention. Tonight, the tastes of peppermint and cream cheese icing still lingered on his tongue, as though he were a second helping of their decadent dessert.

She put her everything into the kiss, pouring her disbelief, her gratitude, her love and her need for him into her touch. Kal's fingers gripped her hips, tugging the skirt higher until he had handfuls of bare flesh. He bit at his lip and groaned as she shifted her weight and made contact with the firm heat of his desire for her.

He tore his lips away from hers at last so he could bury his face in her cleavage. Kal licked at her nipples through the lace, teasing them with the rough fabric. Then he tugged the cups down until her breasts spilled out. He drew one nipple, then the other, into his mouth, teasing with his tongue until she gasped aloud. In the small cabin of the car, every noise seemed incredibly loud, but with just the two of them out here, she could make as much noise as she wanted to. No babies would wake up and no nannies or brothers would overhear.

"You are so beautiful," he murmured against her skin before he planted kisses on the inner curves of her breasts. "I don't know how I managed to resist you for the last three years." Kal's hand cupped one breast and squeezed it gently. "How in the hell am I supposed to just stop wanting you when all this is over?"

That was a good question. It was one Lana wasn't able to answer. If she knew how to flip off her emotions like a light switch, she would feel a lot better about her feelings for Kal. It wasn't going to be that easy, though. He might want her, but she was in love with him. That would be far harder to overcome. Like with all his other relationships, he would move on and forget about her in the arms of another woman. She didn't think that would work very well for her. Dating was a far-off prospect once the divorce was final.

"You'll find someone else to warm your bed," she whispered as she reached down and stroked him through his trousers. "Someone prettier or smarter or more interesting will distract you and then you'll wonder why you were attracted to me."

Kal stiffened beneath her touch, eventually reaching for her wrist and pulling her hand away. "Why would you say that?" he asked.

Lana looked at him and sighed. "Because it's true. It might not be the sexiest thing to say in the moment, but you and I both know that you'll move on from this like you always do. Me...this marriage...it will all become a fuzzy memory after a while. I recommend you do your best to study my body while you have the chance." She ground her hips into his lap, making his eyes roll back and a growl form in his throat.

"I might move on, but there's no way I'll forget you, Lana. I already know every curve of your body like the back of my hand. I know how you like to be touched. What makes you squirm. What makes you scream. That's ingrained in my brain for always."

Hearing those words from him was like a dream and a nightmare all at once. How could he say things like that, want her the way he did, but not have any feelings for her? Those were the kinds of things you said to a woman you wanted to be yours for always, but he had no intention of keeping her in his bed forever.

Lana would make herself crazy if she overthought this. She just needed to treasure the moment, treasure tonight, so she would have it in her memory long after he'd moved on without her. "Then make me scream now," she said.

Kal's jaw clenched and he exhaled loudly in response. Reaching down, he hit the button to recline the passenger seat. Lana moved back with him. The incline was just enough to lift her hips. He slipped his hands up under her skirt and felt for her panties. He clenched the fabric in his fist and gave a tug, ripping them from her hips.

Lana gasped in surprise. "In a hurry?" she asked.

"There's not enough room to maneuver. I'll buy you ten new pairs to replace them."

He shifted beneath her, undoing his pants and sliding them out of the way. With all the barriers gone, he sheathed in latex and found his home inside her, and she was ready for him. She shifted her weight back, taking him deeper with a sigh of contentment. Having her body wrapped around him in such an intimate way made her feel like, for that moment, Kal was all hers. With his ring on her finger and his need for her buried deep inside, it truly felt like they belonged to each other.

At the very least, she was his, even if he could never be hers.

Kal pressed his fingertips deep into the flesh of her hips and rocked her body back and forth. They moved together as the tension built and the windows of the Mercedes fogged up. Lana closed her eyes and tried to absorb every sensation of them together. The scents of leather and sex hung heavy in the air, and the sounds he made were like an arrow straight to her core. He was louder tonight, free to moan, free to whisper erotic words of encouragement when she moved just right.

Then he slipped his hand between them. His fingers sought out her moist center and stroked her there. With every thrust, he rubbed her most sensitive spot, urging her closer and closer to reaching her release. Her cries grew louder. His touch became harder. His hips rose off the seat of the car to pound into her body with the fury of need.

When Lana opened her eyes, Kal was watching her. His dark brown and gold gaze was fixed on her face, watching her every expression. He looked at her as though she were the sexiest, most desirable woman he'd ever seen. He didn't look away, even as his own release grew closer. In the moment, he wasn't closing his eyes and thinking of anything but her.

That put her over.

Bracing her hands on the driver's seat and the door, she thrust her hips hard against him and came undone. Her whole body shuddered with the force of her orgasm as it exploded inside her, her loud cries interrupted by her ragged, gasping breaths. "Oh, Kal," she said, nearly groaning his name as the pleasure continued to ripple through her body.

"Lana," he hissed between clenched teeth. He thrust hard into her from below, and then he lost it. His back arched up off the seat, his jaw dropping open. He shouted her name the second time as he poured into her.

He reached for Lana and pulled her down to lie against his chest as they both recovered. Kal wrapped his arms protectively around her and hugged her tight. She was happy to press her ear against the faint, dark curls of his chest hair and listen to the rapid sound of his heartbeat as it slowly returned to normal.

It felt so normal, so right to be in Kal's arms like this. She didn't want to imagine a time where the man she loved was out of her reach. But it was coming. Before she knew it, all of this would be over.

Ten

The phone rang and Lana lunged to answer it before it woke Akela from her nap. She didn't recognize the number. "Hello?"

"Hello. Lana?" a hesitant woman's voice replied. It sounded familiar and yet she couldn't place it either.

"This is she."

"This is Mele."

Lana felt a twinge of guilt at not knowing the sound of her own sister's voice, but it was different. She sounded...sober. Serious. Those were two things Mele rarely was. "Hi," Lana replied, not quite sure what to say to her. They hadn't spoken since before the arrest. At first, Lana had been too angry, then too concerned about Akela to try and contact her. Then, the drug program the judge sent her to had strict rules about communication with the outside, so Mele either couldn't call or hadn't felt the need to before now.

"How's Akela?" Mele asked in a small, quiet voice.

"She's doing great." Lana wasn't about to sugarcoat this. Her sister needed to know that her daughter was thriving outside the environment she'd lived in with Mele and Tua. "She's got a bottom tooth coming in."

"Really? Wow. Her first tooth." Mele sounded sad about missing her daughter's milestones. It was as though she cared. For Akela's sake, Lana hoped she truly did.

"What took you so long to check on her?" Lana asked, unable and unwilling to keep the cold tone from her voice. It had been almost a month. "She could've been in foster care all this time and you wouldn't have known."

"They told me she was with you, so I knew she was in good hands. I needed to focus on getting better for her."

"And how is that going?" Lana tried not to be pessimistic about her sister's recovery, but it wasn't easy to clean up. It took some addicts several rounds of treatment if they were even able to kick it at all. Some didn't.

"Really well," Mele said in a surprisingly upbeat tone. "Today is the last day of treatment. They'll drug-test me this afternoon, and if I pass—and I will—I'll be released tomorrow."

Tomorrow? It seemed like Akela had just come to live with them, but if Mele was getting released, twenty-eight days had gone by. How was that possible?

Lana knew she should be happy for her sister, but she felt her stomach sink as she realized what Mele was really telling her. She'd completed the program and the judge was letting her out. That meant she would be coming for her daughter. That meant that the reason for her marriage to Kal was coming to an end. That meant everything in her life was about to fall apart.

"Good for you," was all she could manage to say.

"You sound doubtful, Lana."

"I'm sorry if I'm not instantly convinced, but you've cleaned up before. How do I know that you'll stay clean this time? I'm not going to just hand Akela over to you to have you go back to using, and neither will the judge."

"I'm glad. She needs as many people in her life as possible that care for her that much. But I'm one of those people, too. If I feel like I'm going to blow it, I'll bring her to you first. I promise. But there's no reason to worry. I'm in a different place now, mentally and emotionally. Tua is in jail and out of my life for good. I'm starting over with new friends that will be better influences. I've cleaned up for good this time, Lana. My probation requires it, and my daughter deserves it. If I fail a random screening, I go to jail and I might lose Akela for good. I'm not going to let that happen. I'm not leaving my baby again."

There was a determination in Mele's voice that Lana had never heard before. She really seemed to be changed. The month of treatment had made a difference. Lana felt hopeful for the first time since Akela was born and Mele relapsed.

"I'll be released in the morning. Do you think you could pick me up? Our car is still in the police impound. It's going to take me a while to be able to pay the fine to get it out."

Lana tried not to flinch. Her sister would ask her for money any second now. She just knew it. "I can pick you up."

"Great. Thank you."

Lana waited, but the request didn't come. "How are you going to get the money to get your car back?" she asked. Her sister hadn't held down a real job in years.

"It's part of the continuing outpatient program. I go to group and individual counseling each week, pass my drug tests and they help me find somewhere to live and work. They partner with local businesses to place us in stable jobs."

That wasn't the answer Lana had expected. Mele sounded like she was going to handle her transition all by herself. Lana was impressed. She was still hesitant to believe this program had worked a miracle, but it was sounding that way.

"Kal's hotel is actually one of the companies. I was going to see about a housekeeping job there, perhaps. Maybe I could work my way up to something better after a while. Do you think you could talk to him about it?"

Lana bit at her lip. She hated to ask him to do anything else after all he'd done. Mele had no idea what lengths Kal had gone to for her daughter. But she knew he'd do it. Getting her in a stable job and away from Tua was the best thing they could do to keep her from relapsing. "I'll talk to him when he gets home tonight."

"Okay. Well, I'd better get off the phone. But before I do, I want to say thank you, Lana."

"Thank you for what?" she asked.

"For everything." There was a moment of silence that lingered between the sisters. "I'll call you tomorrow morning."

The line disconnected and Lana was left staring in astonishment at her phone. She wasn't sure quite what to do. Part of her was still in disbelief that the conversation had actually happened. She'd gone into this situation knowing it could be over in a month when her sister was released, but deep down, not believing it would happen.

And yet it did. The sick feeling of dread in her stomach confirmed it. She looked up from the table into the living room. The Christmas tree was gone along with most of the decorations, but she'd left the lights up for New Year's Eve. Soon everything would come down and be put away, along with the phony life she was living.

This wasn't her husband, her child or her home. It was all a carefully crafted ruse that was coming to an end. Akela would go back to her mother. With the baby gone, there was no reason to continue the marriage or to live together. At least, not any reason based on how they'd gone into this agreement.

Unfortunately she'd been foolish enough to let herself develop feelings for Kal, even knowing this day would come. She would happily continue things the way they were, even with Akela gone, but she had no way of knowing if he felt anything more than physical attraction for her. There were moments when she thought she saw the glimmer of something like love in his eyes, but she couldn't be sure.

He didn't want to marry, so why would he agree to stay married? Especially to someone like her? He deserved better than her.

Lana dreaded having to tell him. She didn't want to let all this go. At the same time, she couldn't just sit around this afternoon and wait for him to come home to find out.

"Sonia, I'm heading over to the hotel," she said.

The nanny just waved her off as she grabbed her bag and jumped into her new Mercedes. She buzzed through the winding streets of the resort, parking in the back area where the employees left their cars.

"You're early for rehearsal today," the security guard noted as she went through the back door.

"You didn't see their miserable performance last night," Lana answered with a smile. She hoped it sounded authentic and that her breaking heart wasn't audible to passersby.

She found Kal in his office, mindlessly typing away at something. He was just going about his day as he always did, with no idea she was about to drop a bomb on him.

He looked up in surprise and smiled when he saw it was her standing there. "Hey. I was just thinking about lunch if you want to join me."

Lana bit at her lip and shook her head. "That's, uh, not why I came over. I just got a call from Mele."

Kal's dark eyebrows drew together in concern. "Is everything okay?"

"Yeah. Great. Amazing, actually. So great she's getting out tomorrow." She barely got the words out before tears started threatening in her eyes.

Kal leaped out of his chair in alarm and wrapped his arms around her. He let her cry for a good minute before he spoke. "Did she say anything about the judge and the guardianship agreement?"

"She said she had to pass one more drug screening tonight and it was done. She intends to pick Akela up as soon as she gets out."

Kal's strong embrace stiffened around her. She understood his reaction. He loved that baby. She had become his everything.

Lana only wished that he loved her that much.

Kal was a ball of nervous energy. Not since his parents died had he felt so helpless. He was used to being in control of every detail of his life, but this was one thing he couldn't change. The judge's decree was official—Mele had met all the terms of her plea deal and custody of her daughter was restored.

Lana had gone to pick up her sister at the rehabilitation center. Kal had remained behind to watch Akela. It was Lana's suggestion so they could have a little more time together. Once they'd delivered the bad news to Sonia, they'd let her off to search for a new position, so it was just the two of them. With no baby, there was no need for a nanny. Or a nursery. Or a marriage.

Kal sat cross-legged on the floor watching Akela play with her taggie bear. He'd dressed her in a cute little white eyelet dress that had ducks on it. She hadn't liked it, but he also put on socks and white Mary Jane shoes. He wanted her to look like the perfect little princess she was when she went home today.

By the door was a bag packed with things for the baby. The rehab center had arranged for Mele to get an apartment at a nearby complex. He'd supplied a room at the resort for a few days while she picked up some furnishings and got settled in. He'd gotten her hired on in the housekeeping department, so being close would allow her to start working.

Once she was settled into her new place, he would have all the nursery furniture sent there. Akela's clothes, supplies and blankets were in the suitcase to leave with her today. He'd damn near gotten teary packing up that bag.

Akela looked up at him with a wide, one-toothed grin and chubby cheeks, and he felt the center of his chest start to contract as though it were a black hole sucking all his feelings into it. He'd never wanted a family or children, but he never imagined it would be this hard to let this little girl go. She was one of the reasons he left work on time every day. She had become his sunshine. And Lana had become his moonlight.

He felt all of it slipping through his fingers.

A sound in the driveway caught his attention. He looked up, listening to the sound of women's voices come nearer. Every muscle in his body tensed. Then the door opened. No monsters stepped inside, just Lana and another woman who looked like a slightly older version of Lana. Her eyes were narrower, like Akela's, and she was almost on the unhealthy side of thin. She didn't look at Kal, though. Her dark eyes sought out her baby the moment she walked in.

"Akela!" she said, dropping to her knees on the floor beside the baby. She scooped her into her arms and held her tight to her chest. Tears flowed down her cheeks, making Kal feel guilty for every thought he'd had about keeping Akela with them instead of her returning to her mother. Akela seemed content in her mother's arms, grabbing a handful of her dark hair and giving a tug.

It was a sweet reunion, but Kal could hardly stomach it. He got up and grabbed his suit coat off the back of the couch. "I'm going to head into the office," he said.

Lana regarded him with concern in her eyes, but she

didn't try to stop him. "Okay. I'm going to take Mele over to the hotel to get her settled," she said.

Fine. Whatever. He just needed to get out of here. He couldn't sit and watch Mele walk out the door with the baby in her arms. He left them, holing himself up in his office for a couple hours. When he finally looked at his watch, it hadn't been a couple hours. It had been seven, and well past the time he normally left.

What reason did he have to go home with Akela gone?

Lana was still there. That was something. But he wouldn't even have that for much longer. He shut down his computer and slipped out. The office area was dark and quiet as he headed out the back door to where he parked. As he pulled up outside his house, it seemed darker than usual.

When he came in the front door, he found Lana sitting at the kitchen counter, holding a glass of wine. She didn't look up when he approached the room.

"Did Mele and Akela get settled in?" he asked.

Lana nodded slowly. "Yes. Thank you for letting her stay there for a few days. Sonia moved out, too. She found another live-in position and they wanted her to start right away."

Kal slumped against the doorway, resting his shoulder on the wall. The emptiness he'd filled with work returned now that he was home and the hollow shell of their house seemed to echo inside him. "It's too quiet in here now," he said.

"I know." Lana rolled the wineglass back and forth between her palms, not drinking it or looking his way. "Quiet is good for thinking, though. I've been doing a lot of thinking today since you left."

That sounded ominous. "About what?" Kal left his spot on the wall and leaned his elbows onto the counter so Lana couldn't avoid him any longer.

"About what happens next. For us."

That was a thought that Kal hadn't really allowed himself to have for more than half a second at a time. It was hard enough to deal with Akela being gone. "I don't think we have to make any decisions right awa—"

"I called Dexter," she said. "He's drawing up the divorce papers. He said we can come by in the morning to sign them and he'll get them filed with the judge. It will take about thirty days to be finalized, but at least the ball will have started rolling."

Even though it was a rational thing to say, Lana's words felt like an emotional sock to the gut. Why was it that he thought he would have to be the one to bring up the inevitable? Why did it bother him that Lana was moving forward to end this? He'd expected that perhaps she would drag her feet. She was the one who wanted to get married after all. And yet here he was, feeling like he was getting dumped for the first time since his freshman year.

"Are you sure we should move so quickly? It's only Mele's first day out of rehab. What if she starts using again in a week? We'll have to get married again. That's a lot of unnecessary hassle. Why don't we wait awhile and see what happens? It's not like either of us needs to run out and marry someone else."

Lana looked at him at last and her delicate brow was furrowed in thought and irritation. "In a week, in a month, in a year...we can't control or anticipate what my sister is going to do and we shouldn't live our lives waiting for the other shoe to drop."

"I'm not saying that. I'm just saying a lot has happened today. Let's not make a knee-jerk decision."

"And do what?" Lana said, perking up in her seat at last. "Stay married? Keep continuing on sleeping together and playing the happy lovers for everyone? We're just torturing ourselves the longer we let this go on."

"I hardly feel tortured being married to you, Lana. It's no hardship on me to continue."

"That's because you're not in l—" She stopped her words short. Her jaw clenched and her nostrils flared with pent up emotions as she seemed to fight to hold them in.

"Not in what?" he pressed.

"In love, Kal. You're not in love with me, so of course this is just some fun game you can play. Play at being married and having a family. It's more fun when you know it will end and things will go back to the way they were before."

In love. Was Lana in love with him? He was stunned nearly speechless by the idea of it. "Hold on. This isn't just a game for me. Why would you think that?"

Lana frowned at him. "Kal, are you in love with me? If you are, say so right now."

Being put on the spot, Kal's lungs seized in his chest. In love? Did he even know what it felt like to be in love with a woman? He didn't know. He knew that he cared for Lana as much as he cared for anyone. Judging by the expression on her face, that wasn't enough for her.

"That says everything," she said, standing up from her barstool.

"Now just wait a minute," Kal argued. "You're not giving me time to think."

Lana just shook her head sadly. "You shouldn't have to think about it, Kal. You either love me or you don't. You either want to stay married or you don't. Since the answer is extremely obvious to me, I say there's no point in dragging this conversation on any longer. It's over. We'll meet with Dexter in the morning."

Kal didn't know what to say. Part of him was relieved to have this all done. He'd been nervous about taking marriage and family on to begin with. The other part of him was screaming inside not to be a fool and ruin the amazing thing they had together. "Lana—"

"Thank you, Kal," Lana interrupted, holding up her hand to silence his argument.

"Thank you for what?"

"For putting your own life on hold for over a month to help me. I'm not sure many friends would've gone to the lengths you went to for me, and I appreciate it."

There was a finality in Lana's voice that he didn't like. As though she were saying goodbye. "I'd do it all over again," he said, and he meant it. He watched as Lana picked up her purse, slung it over her shoulder and walked into the living room. "Where are you going?"

She stopped just short of the front door and reached for the small roller bag he hadn't noticed when he'd come in. Lana was leaving him. She'd spent today thinking while he worked his feelings into submission, and the answer she'd come up with was that they were done. She turned to look at Kal. "I'm going back to my place."

"This is your place," he said firmly.

Lana just shook her head. "Don't worry about having your people pack up my stuff for me yet. I've put a couple things in this bag to last me, but I won't need the rest right away. Today I found a nice studio on the hill in Lahaina that I think I'm going to put an offer on. It would be easier to just have them move my things straight there after I close on it."

She looked down at her hand on the doorknob, then reached for her wedding ring. She pulled it off her finger and set it on the table in the entryway.

Kal had hardly given his wedding ring any notice since the day she'd placed it on his finger. Suddenly the cool metal started to burn his skin. It was like everything was being torn apart and he couldn't stand it. He didn't want to lose all this. He took a few giant steps forward until he was nearly in reach of her. "Ask me again," he demanded.

Lana just looked up at him. "At the moment it hurts. But let's not make that pain out to be more than it really is. You like the idea of what we had, but it won't be the same. This isn't what you wanted for your life, Kal. You did this for me. And if I were to let you stay in the marriage knowing that, I would just be taking advantage of our friendship. I've already done too much of that, so don't ask me to do it again."

Kal's feelings were a jumble inside him. He didn't know how he felt or if she was right. He just knew that he didn't want to lose her. "And what about our friendship?" he asked. It felt like even that was crumbling around him. He feared that more than anything else.

"We're fine," she said, reaching out to give him one of her friendly punches in the shoulder. It felt familiar, like old times, but the faraway look in her eyes as she did it didn't convince him. "I'll just need a little time alone, Kal. I promise."

He was relieved to hear that, and yet the anxiety still kept his chest so tight he could barely breathe.

"Good night, Kal," she said, opening the door and slipping outside.

Kal stood there and watched her pull away in her Jeep, leaving the Mercedes in the garage. He couldn't move, couldn't run after her. She had practically said that she loved him, but she didn't seem like she wanted him to chase her. Had her love for him only made her miserable? Perhaps Kal had been right about relationships all along. They always ended in heartache. Maybe she was right and this was for the best.

Their lives weren't so terrible before. They had fun together. Kids were a big responsibility they didn't need to take on. Marriage was something that other people wanted, not him. If he could adjust to being married with a baby so quickly, he should able to get his life back to normal twice as fast.

Even as he thought that to himself, Kal knew it was a lie.

Eleven

"Do you want me to hang this picture right here?" Lana asked, looking over her shoulder.

Mele came into the living room with Akela on her hip and nodded. "That looks great."

Lana hammered the nail into the wall and hung the painting they'd found at a thrift shop. She took a step back and admired her work with pride. It was really coming along.

Mele's new apartment was nice. It was small, but close to the hotel and therapy. The bedroom was big enough for a full-size bed and Akela's crib. By the time the baby was big enough to need her own room, Mele would hopefully be in better financial shape.

"Thanks for all your help with this," Mele said. She put Akela in her bouncing entertainment center so she could play with all the multicolored trinkets there to amuse her. "I feel like we've spent more time together this week than we have in years."

"That's probably true." Lana hadn't spent much time with her sister after she moved from home. She didn't like being around her friends, and for good reason. Now, with all those influences out of Mele's life, it was like she'd gotten her sister back. When the two of them weren't working, Lana was at her apartment helping her move in. They'd done some thrift store shopping and salvaged a few good items from their old place.

"Do you want some coffee?" Mele asked. She'd used a small portion of her first paycheck to buy an inexpensive coffeemaker at Walmart. It was her new indulgence after setting aside all her other addictions.

"Sure." She joined her sister at the tiny, worn dining room table they'd found at a yard sale for fifty bucks.

They sat quietly sipping their coffee and enjoying each other's company. Lana tried not to think about waking up to a cup from Kal each morning. That just sent her thoughts spiraling down the dark rabbit hole of emotional angst.

Walking away had been the hardest thing she'd ever had to do. But she knew she had to. She loved Kal, but she also loved herself enough to know that she didn't want to settle. If he told her he loved her under pressure like that, she had no reason to think it was how he really felt. Or that he wouldn't recant later when he realized what he'd gotten himself into. She wanted a relationship with a man who knew how he felt and wanted to be with her more than anything else in the world. No question. That just wasn't Kal.

She hadn't seen him since she walked out that night. Lana had opted to go to Dexter's office early the next morning by herself to sign the paperwork and avoid another awkward confrontation. She'd circumvented his normal hunting grounds at the hotel. Somehow it made it easier. She couldn't see him every day and pretend her heart wasn't broken. Perhaps once the divorce was final they could return to being friends again. That was what she'd told him. She just hoped it was true.

"Lana?"

Lana turned to her sister, who had an expectant look on her face. "What?"

"I said your name three times. What planet are you on?"

"I'm sorry. I'm a little distracted today."

Mele nodded. "Is this about Kal?"

Lana sat bolt upright in her chair. "What makes you say that?"

"Because…you haven't mentioned his name all week. When my lawyer told me that my sister and her husband had petitioned for guardianship I kept my mouth shut, but honestly my jaw nearly hit the floor. What is going on with you two?"

Lana twisted her lips in thought as she looked down at her mug. "You don't want to hear my sob story, Mele. We're supposed to be focusing on new starts."

Her sister crossed her arms over her chest and gave her a stern look. "Lanakila, you tell me right now or I'll tug your ear."

Lana looked up with wide eyes at her sister. On more than one occasion when she'd annoyed her older sister, she'd been dragged by the ear into the living room so Mele could tattle to Papa. It usually backfired with both of them being punished. She hadn't tugged on her ear in fifteen years, but Lana could still feel the sharp pinch of her sister's grip. She wasn't looking forward to experiencing that again any time soon. "Okay, fine."

"Start at the beginning. I don't know much about you two and I want every detail."

With a sigh, Lana did as she was told, starting with the day she met Kal and continuing up until the day she walked out. They went through a whole pot of coffee and a breakfast pastry Lana brought from the corner bakery. They even stopped to put Akela down for a nap. The story of Lana and Kal was longer than she had ever expected it to be. They had quite a history together.

"So there you go," she said at last. "I'm in love with my best friend. He doesn't love me. And we're getting divorced in..." She glanced down at her phone. "...twenty-two days."

"Wow," was all Mele could say. She'd asked for the whole story and she'd gotten it. "That's crazy. I got the feeling that you two might be playing some sort of shell game for the judge. I can't believe you two were willing to go to such great lengths for my baby." Her eyes got a little teary as she looked over at the infant who napped in her Pack 'n Play. "You have no idea how much I appreciate everything you two went through for her. I'm worried that you paid too high a price, though."

Lana tried to shrug it off. "It was worth it."

"Was it?"

"Absolutely. I just wish I had known going in that it was going to end like this. I could've protected my heart better. Kept my distance when there wasn't anyone else around. He's just got such a magnetic personality. I'm drawn to him."

"How did you think all this would end?" Mele asked.

"Like this," she had to admit when she really thought about it. She was already half sweet on him going into the situation. Did she really think twenty-four-hour contact, living together, a wedding ring and sex would make him easier to resist? "I can try to blame the heart-break and the attachment on the sex, which wasn't a part of my plan, but I know that wasn't it. In the end, I would've fallen for him no matter what. I just thought I would handle it better. The sex gave me the illusion that he might fall for me, too, which of course is ridiculous."

Mele flinched at her words. "Why on earth would you think it's ridiculous for him to fall in love with you?"

"Oh, come on, Mele."

"Don't *come on* me. What about you is so repellant that he couldn't fall in love with you? You're beauti-ful. You're smart. You're talented. You take care of the people you love, and you love more deeply than anyone I've ever known. He should be thrilled that you'd consider falling in love with him, not the other way around."

"You're crazy. Maybe I'm pretty and I'm a good dancer. So what? Kal is from such an important fam-ily. I think he mentioned once that he's descended from Hawaiian royalty on his mother's side. He has more money in his bank account on any given day than I'll earn in my whole life. He's from a different kind of people. The kind of people who don't fall in love with people like us."

"You mean people like me," Mele said matter-of-factly.

Lana realized after she said it how it might insult

her sister. "That's not what I meant, I'm sorry, but it certainly doesn't help the situation to have an inebriated, violent father and a sister always on the wrong side of the law."

Mele shook her head with a smile. "No, don't apologize. You're right. At least about our family. We're no great name and we'll be lucky to inherit the tiny plot of useless land where Papa's house sits. We've got issues for sure. But everyone does. Some just have more money to deal with their issues. Our family is lucky, though. You know why? Because we have you. You're our diamond in the rough."

Lana was uncomfortable with her sister's flattery. They'd chosen different paths, but she didn't believe that she was better than her sister. "Oh, quit it. I can dance. That's what got me out of our situation. If I'd had two left feet and buckteeth, who knows what would've happened to me?"

Mele furiously shook her head. "No, you never would've ended up like me. You're too much like Mama for that."

Lana looked at her sister with tears suddenly welling in her eyes. "Really?" She'd only turned two a few weeks before their mother died from the cervical cancer they'd discovered while she was in the hospital having Lana. Instead of being home with her new baby, she'd been in and out of treatment, but they'd caught it too late. Lana had no memories of her, just a few worn photos that showed a resemblance, but not much more. Mele had been five and remembered more about those days.

"Absolutely. Why do you think Papa fell apart when she died? Because Mama was everything to him. He would sit and hold you in his arms and cry because he knew she was slipping away and there was nothing he could do about it. He never let himself fall in love with anyone else because of it. He couldn't stand to have his heart broken again when he knew there wasn't anyone who could replace her."

Lana's words jogged something in her memory. It was something Kal had said once, a long time ago. The night had possibly involved beer, which was the usual catalyst for loosening Kal's tongue about personal matters. He'd said falling in love was too big a risk. That he knew what it was like to lose someone he loved and he didn't understand how she could long for a husband and a family when it could be ripped away at any moment.

"That sounds like Kal," she said aloud.

"What does?"

"What you just said about Papa. Kal lost his parents about ten years ago. He doesn't talk about it very much, but I can tell that it really bothers him, even now. It makes me wonder if that's why…"

"Why he's afraid to admit that he's in love with you?"

Lana shook her head and frowned. "I was going to say that was why he was afraid to be in a serious relationship. Why would you think he's in love with me?" That was quite a stretch, especially for someone who'd only seen him for a handful of minutes and didn't even speak with him. Lana had spent almost every minute of the last month with him and she didn't believe that was true.

Mele stood up and started another pot of coffee. "If everything you've told me about Kal is true, he has to be in love with you."

"Why?"

"Because he's not a fool. He's smart. He's a successful businessman who's used to having everything work out the way he wants it to. But you can't control love the way you control a business empire, and he knows that. He might be scared of admitting the truth to you and getting hurt, but he's not a fool."

Kal was sulking. He wouldn't admit it to anyone else, but he was. At first, he thought he was just missing the baby. And he was. But that wasn't what was haunting him. It was Lana's disappointed face he saw when he closed his eyes to sleep at night. Lana's laughter that he missed when he saw something that they would've had a good time talking about. Lana's lips that he fantasized about kissing.

He missed her. It had been over a week since he'd even seen her. No calls, no texts, no passing in the lobby of the hotel. It was just like she'd vanished from his life entirely, even though she was probably only a couple hundred yards away at any given time.

Kal supposed that if he really wanted to see her, he could watch the luau. But he hadn't been able to bring himself do it. Watching her dance would just torture him even more. Maybe tonight. Or maybe not.

"Mr. Bishop?"

Kal looked up from his desk to see his assistant, Jane, standing in the doorway of his office. "Yes?"

"There's someone here to see you, sir."

"Someone here to see me?"

"Well, not *see* you, per se," a man's voice said as the door flew open the rest of the way, revealing Mano and Hōkū standing behind her. "But we're here to visit."

Kal stood up in surprise. It was weird enough that Mano had shown up for Christmas. This random Monday in January visit was unheard of. He waited to respond until Mano had settled down in a guest chair and Jane had disappeared, closing the door behind her.

"What are you doing here?" he asked. "No bullshit this time."

"Okay, fine. I'm here because your employees are worried about you and they contacted me."

Kal nearly tipped his chair backward in surprise. He surged forward and gripped his desk to stay steady. "You're kidding, right?"

"Nope. Apparently you've been charging up and down the halls like a man on fire, barking orders, criticizing everyone's work and being a general pain in the a—"

"Okay," Kal said, interrupting him. "I get it. I've been unpleasant." He knew he'd been in a bad mood, but he hadn't realized how bad. "Did someone really call you and ask you to come?"

"Actually they asked for permission to slip you a sedative in your morning coffee, so I thought me coming out here was a better solution."

Kal crossed his arms defensively over his chest. "I'll work on it. It's been a bad week."

Mano nodded thoughtfully, then reached out to feel Kal's left hand. "That's what I thought. No ring," he noted.

Kal pulled his hand away and gazed down at the naked ring finger of his left hand. He'd only worn the ring for a month, but he could feel the phantom sensation of it on his finger even with it gone. "No ring," he repeated. "No marriage. No baby. It's all over and done."

"What happened?"

He sighed, not really wanting to admit the truth to his brother but knowing he had to. "You were right about the two of us. None of it was real. We had to let everyone believe it was in case Child Services was sniffing around, but it was all for show. Lana's sister went into rehab and it was the only way we could get guardianship of her niece. Her sister has since completed treatment and has been reunited with her daughter. So it's done. Lana left."

Mano listened, making that infuriatingly thoughtful face that always made Kal nervous. He'd always heard that losing one sense made the others stronger. His brother had picked up some kind of superpower lie detector in the accident that blinded him.

"You mean you let her go," Mano said at last.

"No, I mean she called the lawyer, started the divorce proceedings and moved out." That was all true. Aside from the teeny, tiny detail about her asking if he loved her and him choking.

"It seems strange to me that a woman so obviously in love with her husband would just walk out like that. It sounds to me like self-preservation. What did you do to her?"

"I didn't do anything to her," Kal argued. "I stuck to the agreement. She's the one who broke the rules."

"And what, exactly, were the rules?"

"That it was just for show. That it was just for the baby and nothing more."

"So you didn't sleep with her?"

Kal was starting to feel like he'd woken up in the

Spanish Inquisition. When he found out who had called his brother on him, he was going to show them what a grumpy manager he really could be. "Yes, I slept with her."

"More than once?"

Kal gritted his teeth. "Yes, damn it."

"So you broke the rules, too?"

He supposed that he did. "Yes. We broke that rule. But she wasn't supposed to get attached, and it wasn't supposed to ruin our friendship."

Mano nodded and reached over to pat the top of Hōkū's head. "So you spent a month together playing house, making love and acting like a happy family for everyone, and now you're mad at her because she fell for you in the process."

"Yes."

"Or," Mano postulated, "are you mad at yourself because you fell for her, too?"

Kal closed his eyes and groaned aloud. He did not want to have this conversation with his brother, but he could tell there was no getting out of it. "This is a conversation better suited for the bar," he said. "I need a drink."

Mano smiled cheerfully and stood up. "Lovely. I could use a drink myself."

They made their way to the bar and found a dark corner booth. It was too early for most drinkers, so they had the place to themselves. Once they were settled with beverages and a bowl of Asian snack mix, Mano sat back and waited for the answer Kal had stalled responding to for ten minutes.

"I'm not in love," Kal said at last.

Mano just sighed. "You know, it wasn't that long ago

that I was sitting at Tūtū Ani's birthday party while you talked me into chasing after the woman I loved but had let walk out of my life."

"That was different," Kal insisted. "You *were* in love with her."

"And you can honestly say that you have no feelings for Lana?"

Kal tried to search himself for something he was hiding, but he didn't come up with anything novel. "I feel the same way for Lana that I've always felt. She's my best friend. I enjoy spending time with her, and I miss her when I don't see her often enough. I like sharing things with her, and I can tell her anything. She's great to talk to and always gives good advice."

"If you were in this situation with another woman and you asked Lana for advice, what would she say?"

He knew the answer immediately. He could even hear her say it in his head. "She'd tell me to get my head out of my ass and tell the woman that I love her."

"Considering that you say nothing has changed, is it possible that you're confused about your feelings for her because you've been in love with her all along?"

His brother's words stopped him cold. He gazed silently down into his drink as though the answers to the universe were there among the ice and the scotch. Was it really possible that he'd been in love with her all this time? Was that why he was never interested in anyone else? Why he'd rather spend time with her than go on a date? Why he was terrorizing his employees since she'd walked out on him? The answer washed over him like a tidal wave of emotion that made the hairs stand up on the back of his neck and his chest ache with his foolishness.

His head dropped into his hand and he clutched his skull to keep his mind from being blown. "Oh my God, I've been in love with her the whole time."

"Yep," was all Mano said. He reached a hand out to feel for the snack bowl and grabbed a handful of sesame sticks and peanuts. Kal watched him pop a bit into his mouth as though they were discussing the weather.

"I'm in love with Lana," he said aloud, letting his ears get used to the sound of it. If he ever said it to her, he couldn't have the slightest hesitation or she wouldn't believe him. He certainly hadn't given her any reason to believe him before.

He replayed their last moments together again in his mind, thinking about how she'd looked at him with her heart wide-open and he'd blown it. She'd been right, though. If he'd told her he loved her then, it would've been just lip service to keep her from walking away. Being apart from her this last week had cemented it in his mind. Now he understood the truth of his feelings.

All this time he'd been afraid to get close to anyone and risk losing them, and here he'd gone and pushed away the only person he'd ever loved. The result was the same—he was alone and miserable. The only difference was that he still had a chance to make things right with Lana.

He had to tell her how he felt and stand his ground. He wasn't going to let her walk away this time, or ever again. She was still legally his wife and he wasn't about to let that change.

"Now the question is, what are you going to do about it?"

Twelve

It was Lana's turn to go on. The lights dimmed for a moment and the musicians started chanting an ancient Hawaiian prayer as they beat their drums. She stepped onto the stage, finding her mark in the center before the spotlights focused on her.

Lana had performed this routine three nights a week for three years. She knew it like the back of her hand, and yet she felt sluggish as she started to move. One of her professors in college had told her that she danced with her whole heart and soul. Her heart just wasn't in it lately.

She pasted a smile on her face and fought through it. She'd performed with the flu, she'd performed with a sprained ankle—she could get through this. That was what professionals did.

Instinctively she looked to the far corner of the courtyard as she danced. That was where Kal had watched her every night for as long as she could remember. He wasn't there now and he hadn't been since she moved out. Lana supposed that was her fault. She told him she needed space and he was giving it to her.

Still, it hurt her heart to look up and see nothing but a stone wall where his tall, dark silhouette should be.

Mele had insisted that Kal wasn't a fool and that he would come around. Lana wasn't so sure. Their father had never recovered and moved on; why did she think that Kal would change his ways after all these years? And for her of all people?

She closed her eyes for a moment and forced that negative thought from her mind. If she got nothing else from her time with Mele, it was that she was a valuable person. She needed to stop thinking she wasn't good enough. She was her mother's daughter, and every time she let those negative thoughts creep in, she was tarnishing her mother's memory. She couldn't allow that.

Better to believe that Kal was a fool if he didn't see what a gem he had right in front of him. Lana wasn't going to sit around and wait for him to change his mind, either. She was going to buy that condo, move out of the hotel and start building a life that didn't revolve around him and his resort. She'd actually heard that one of the big luaus in Lahaina was hiring a choreographer. It was a scary thought to leave the place she'd considered home, but maybe it was time.

Her eyes drifted over to the corner even as she considered leaving the Mau Loa. This time, she was startled to see a familiar dark shape. Kal was there. Watching her.

Missing a step, she forced herself to focus back on her performance. When she looked up again, Kal was gone. Her heart ached with disappointment. She couldn't take much more of this. She had to go, she decided. She had to get away from him if she was ever going to be able to move on with her life.

The routine came to an end. The lights went out, allowing her to leave the stage just as the male dancers came rushing out. Turning the corner, she ran face first into Talia, one of her dancers.

"We've got a problem, Lana."

Lana's stomach started aching with dread. "What is it?"

"Callie is puking her guts up in the rehearsal room. There's no way she's going to be able to perform the new *South Pacific* number at the end of the show."

Damn it. That was a really important number, and a relatively new one she performed with one of the male singers from the band. She didn't really have an understudy yet, so that meant that Lana would have to do it. Her worries about Kal faded into the background as she rushed around making last-minute arrangements for the change. "Go over to the band area and let Ryan know that I'm taking Callie's place."

Talia nodded and headed off toward the pit where the musicians sat just to the right of the stage. Lana returned to the dressing room to change out of her current outfit and into Callie's costume. It was a flowing white dress that was paired with a crown of white orchids. It pained Lana to put it on, reminding her too much of her wedding dress. As performance after performance went by, she fidgeted nervously in the dress.

She couldn't wait for the new number to be over with so she could take the costume off.

Finally the last routine of the night was up and she went out to do her job. She stepped out onto the stage first. The setup was a little different from their usual numbers. Ryan would step out behind her and while she danced, sing the song "Some Enchanted Evening" from the musical *South Pacific*. It had been an instant hit with the audience, and gave them the chance to showcase Ryan's singing talents.

Thankfully Lana didn't have to sing. She just had to dance, and in the end, end up in Ryan's arms just before the lights went out. It was a simple dance number, drawing more on her background in contemporary and ballet dance than her hula skills.

The musicians started playing the acoustic guitar version of the song and Lana waited for her cue to begin dancing. She stared out into the crowd, trying not to look for Kal. Then Ryan began singing and her blood went cold. Something was wrong. That wasn't Ryan's voice. It was pleasant enough, and relatively on-key, but it lacked the professional vocal tones of a trained singer like Ryan.

Unfortunately she couldn't turn around. She didn't turn in the performance for a full minute. She danced, listening to him sing about spying her across a crowded room and being enchanted by her.

Then, at last, the routine allowed her to stop and turn to look at her partner. It was Kal, wearing the white linen suit Ryan typically wore.

She froze in place. He was standing there, crooning words of love to her. Lana couldn't make sense of what she was seeing. What was he doing crashing the luau? She hadn't even seen Kal in over a week and now he just appeared in her show without telling her? Lana didn't even know Kal could sing. What was going on?

Either way, she told herself it didn't matter. She would finish this number, then drag him backstage and give him a sound talking-to for putting her on the spot like this. She reached out to him longingly, then turned away and spun across the stage with the dress twirling around her.

She dreaded the final chorus of the song, knowing she would have to look lovingly into Kal's eyes as he serenaded her. If ever there was a time she would blow her professional facade, it would be now.

He started the last verse and she slowly made her way to him. She swallowed hard as she looked into his eyes and saw the serious expression on his face. It was as though he meant every word as he sang to her about finding his true love and flying to her side. She tried not to read too much into it, though. These were Rogers and Hammerstein's words, not Kal's.

As he wrapped his arms around her, he looked down at her as though they weren't onstage surrounded by hundreds of people. He sang the last few lines of the song to her, looking deep into her eyes.

The music faded and the crowd broke into roaring applause. Lana expected him to let go of her, but he didn't. Instead he said, "I don't want to go through my life dreaming alone. I want to go through it with you."

Lana didn't know what to say, and even if she did, she didn't want to speak it aloud. Kal was miked, and everything he said was broadcast to the whole audience. "You don't really mean that, Kal," she whispered, hoping it wouldn't pick up her voice.

"If I didn't mean it, would I be onstage, singing to you and making a fool of myself? Would I have convinced your dancers to fake being sick to make sure you were the one to perform this song?"

It was a setup. Lana turned her head and noticed her entire dance crew, including a quite healthy Callie, watching anxiously from the backstage area. Lana squeezed her eyes closed and tried to wrap her head around what was happening. So was the crowd. The courtyard was so quiet you could hear the waves beyond the stage.

"I went to all this trouble because I wanted to tell you, to tell everyone here tonight, how much I love you, Lana."

She shook her head in disbelief. "You could've just told me this in private."

"You and I both know that wouldn't work. I wanted witnesses. I wanted you to know I mean business. And I didn't want you to be able to run away so you'd have to listen to what I have to say."

Lana was stiff in his arms. He was right to put her on the spot so she couldn't avoid him, but onstage?

"I'm not letting you get rid of me," Kal said. "This last week without you has been pure hell. I don't want to go back to the way things were. I don't want to live in that big house all alone. I want a family. A real one, like my brother has and my parents had. And I want it with you."

"You don't mean that. You're just confusing our friendship for something more."

"You are my friend. You're my best friend. But

you're also the love of my life and I'm not confused about that. I'm not going to settle for anything less than you as my wife for the rest of my life."

Kal's words stole her breath away. With his arms wrapped around her and his eyes pleading with her to love him in return, she didn't know how she could tell him no. But she summoned the strength anyway.

"You've lost your mind. Let go of me," she said angrily, pulling from his arms and running offstage.

The minute Lana turned to Kal while she was dancing and realized it was him singing, he knew he had made a mistake. There was a hardness in her gaze, a stiffness in the set of her jaw. He'd thought that a big, romantic, public gesture would be the way to go. That declaring his love for her in front of everyone would convince her that he meant what he said, but as she ran offstage and the audience audibly gasped at her rebuttal, he knew it was the wrong tactic to take with Lana.

He ran after her, pushing through the crowds of dancers and chasing her down the sandy path that led to the beach. "Lana!" he shouted, hearing his voice echo through the speakers in the distance. He ripped off his microphone and tossed it into the bushes as he chased her down the beach. "Lana, wait!"

She finally came to a stop at the edge of the water. She stood there, with her back to him, as he slowly approached.

"Lana?"

She finally turned to look at him. Her face was flushed and her eyes were glassy with unshed tears. "How dare you!" she shouted.

Kal froze. He wasn't expecting her anger. "What do you mean?"

"How dare you make me look like a fool in front of all those people!"

"You didn't look like a fool! I made myself look like one to try and prove to you how much I love you."

Lana could only shake her head. "In front of my dance team, in front of the hotel guests…"

"Who all thought it was an amazing and romantic gesture. They were all superexcited to help me out. And the audience loved it until you ran away and ruined everything."

"What made you think that putting me on the spot was the right thing to do?" she asked. "Even if I was in love with you, I'm a very private person, Kal. And a professional. I don't like my personal life bleeding into my work like that."

Kal sighed and closed his eyes. "I'm sorry, Lana. I should've known better." He took a few steps closer to her, closing the gap to inches. "I'd just seen them perform that song at the last luau, and it seemed so perfect. The man knows he has to act now if he doesn't want to lose his chance to be with the woman he loves. That was what I was doing. I wanted to sing those words to you so you'd know they were true."

Lana's expression softened. "You've been watching the show? I haven't seen you."

Kal nodded, pleased that Lana had noted his absence. She was annoyed with him, but she *had* been watching for him at each performance. That was something. "I've been sitting in the audience instead so you wouldn't see me."

Lana sighed, her shoulders relaxing along with the

rest of her tense muscles. "I thought you'd stopped coming to watch us dance."

He shook his head. "I did for the first one, but I realized that I couldn't stay away, even though I knew you wanted me to. I'm in love with you, Lana. Whether or not we have an audience, what I have to say to you is the same."

"I don't believe you," she said. "I think you're just lonely and scrambling to keep me in your life. Please don't tell me you love me unless you absolutely mean it. My heart can't take it, Kal, if you change your mind."

"This isn't a new feeling, Lana, it's just a new revelation. Since you've been gone, I realized that my feelings didn't change for you after we married or after we broke up. At first I thought that meant that I didn't have romantic feelings for you. But then I realized that it was because I've been in love with you this whole time."

Lana's lips parted softly in surprise. He wanted to scoop her into his arms and kiss her, but he refrained, since his last romantic gesture had crashed and burned.

"What do you mean, 'this whole time'?"

"I mean I've been in love with you for three years. All this time you were the most important person in my life, my best friend, the one I wanted to share things with, but I was too stubborn to realize that it was more than friendship. I wasn't interested in a relationship with anyone else because it wasn't a relationship with you."

"But you don't want to get married or have a family."

"I was scared to get married and have a family. Scared to lose the one I loved. Then I realized I'd lost you anyway. I couldn't bring my parents back, but I could do something about this. I could tell you how I felt and pray that you believed me."

"You really do love me," Lana said with a touch of disbelief in her voice.

"I do. And I want to stay married to you, as well. I've called Dexter and told him to postpone the divorce proceedings."

Lana just looked at him as though he'd sprouted a second head. She glanced up at his hairline, reaching out to gently brush some of his hair out of his face. "Did you hit your head or something?"

Kal grasped her hand and tugged it to his chest. "Of course not. This isn't a concussion talking, this is me, being honest with myself, and being honest with you, for the first time. Now I want you to be honest with me."

"About what?" she asked.

"I've been pretty clear about my feelings. What about you? Do you love me, Lana?"

She bit nervously at her bottom lip before she nodded. "I do."

Kal broke into a wide grin. He pulled her closer to him. "And do you want to marry me?"

"We're already married, Kal."

He reached into his pocket and fished out the platinum band she'd left behind. "Then I guess you'd better put on your wedding ring."

Lana took a ragged breath and held her fingers outstretched for Kal to slip the ring onto her finger.

"That's not all," he said. Reaching into his pocket again, he pulled out a jewelry box. He opened the lid and held his breath for her response.

"Kal!" she gasped. "I told you I didn't need a diamond ring."

He plucked the ring out of the velvet bed and slipped
it onto her finger with the wedding band. The ring was
a uniquely Hawaiian design from a local artisan, with
an oval diamond set in a band of curling platinum vines
and Plumeria flowers. It rested perfectly against her
wedding band, as it was designed to do.

"You didn't need a diamond when we were getting
married for the judge. Now that you're going to be my
wife for real, and for always, you need a diamond ring
to prove it."

Lana admired her rings, then placed her hand on his
chest and looked up at him. "We don't have to prove
our love to anyone anymore. It's just for us."

"Well, there are a few people who would like to
know that we're in love and happy and staying married."

"Like who?"

Kal took her hand and started leading her back
across the beach toward the stage. As they got closer,
the sound of the conch shell being blown echoed
through the night. Kal loved the puzzled look on
Lana's face that stayed there until they stepped out
onto the stage again.

The whole audience was still seated, waiting anxiously for their return. The dancers were sitting in the
audience and with the houselights on, Kal could see
Mano and Paige sitting up front. He'd wanted them
to be here for this, since they'd missed the first ceremony. Right beside them was Mele holding Akela,
and Lana's father.

Lana noticed her family sitting there where she

hadn't seen them before. She tugged at his arm, stopping him short. "What is going on?"

Kal stepped to the side and the kahuna *pule* who married them the first time was standing in the middle of the stage. Her eyes grew wide; then she looked back at Kal. "We're renewing our vows," he explained.

"Here? Right now?"

"Why not? You're practically in a wedding dress. Our family is here. The holy man is here. We also have three hundred guests who are anxiously waiting to see us kiss so they can eat the wedding cake at our reception."

"Our reception?"

Kal pointed to the far side of the courtyard where a table was set up to display a beautiful, five-tiered wedding cake covered in purple and white orchids. "We didn't have any of this the first time because it wasn't for real, we were just checking the box. Now that we're staying married, I wanted to have something a little grander to commemorate our vow renewal."

Lana looked around at everyone in the audience. They watched them with silent, expectant faces. "I can't believe you did all this. How did you...? When did you...?"

Kal just shook his head. That was a story for another time. Right now they had a wedding to attend. "So, what do you say we get remarried, Mrs. Bishop?"

Before she could respond, the crowd started to cheer. The roar of applause, whistles and shouts made her cheeks flush bright red. Finally she looked at him and nodded, eliciting another round of cheers.

Kal took her hand and led her to the table where the kahuna *pule* was waiting for them. He opened up his prayer booklet to the marked page and started reciting the words he'd just spoken to them a month before.

"The Hawaiian word for love is aloha. Today we've come together to celebrate the special aloha that exists between you, Kalani and Lanakila, as you renew your vows of marriage. When two people promise to share the adventure of life together, it is a beautiful moment that they will always remember."

They repeated their vows, and this time when they kissed, there was no awkwardness or hesitation. He wrapped his arms around Lana and dipped her backward, drawing a roar of applause from the crowd. They embraced their family members and cut the cake so it could be served to the hotel guests who were, in a way, an extension of their family.

It was late when Kal finally pulled the Jaguar back up to the house. He surprised Lana again by scooping her out of her seat and carrying her across the threshold.

They stood there together in their home with Lana in his arms. "I can't believe any of this is happening," she said. "You are amazing. You put all this together just for me."

"Of course I did. I told you I loved you. I wanted you to have everything you could possibly want. Except for maybe a few surprises so you'd go along with it all. What did you think when you turned around and saw me on the stage?"

Lana arched her brow at him. "Do you really want to know?"

"Of course I do."

"I was thinking that you were a terrible singer."

Kal looked at his wife in mock horror. "You lie!" he

said as he carried her down the hall to the master bed-room. "You're going to pay for that tonight," he said with a wicked grin.

Lana smiled and kissed him with all the passion she could muster. "I hope so."

Epilogue

Lana had to admit she was a little jealous of Mano and Paige's new house. The sprawling house sat atop a cliff overlooking the sea on the eastern side of Oahu. Diamondhead was visible to the right and in front of them was just miles of beautiful blue sea.

It was the perfect backdrop for their wedding. The rain had held out for a lovely Valentine's Day ceremony. Paige had looked beautiful in a pale cream, almost rose colored lace gown. Her hair was swept back in a romantic chignon with pale pink hibiscus woven into it. Her baby bump was on full display and all of Mano's relatives had to keep touching it as though she were a good-luck Buddha statue.

Mano was beaming in his traditional white suit. Hōkū was dressed up, too, with a matching white bow tie, since he was officially the ring bearer for the ceremony.

It all worked out splendidly, which made Lana happy considering how stressed Paige had been over the whole thing. All things considered, Lana was actually happy that her two wedding ceremonies had been virtually spur-of-the-moment with little to no planning on her part. In the end, she'd gotten the dress and the man of her dreams, and that was all she really needed.

"Lana?"

Lana turned to see Kal and Mano's elderly grandmother, Ani, making her way over to her. "Aloha, Tūtū Ani."

The older woman smiled and took her hand. "I had a dream last night that I must tell you about."

Lana looked over at the nearby table. "Let's have a seat and you can tell me all about it." Ani looked like she could use a rest, and frankly so could Lana. It had been a long day and she was pretty tired from all the celebrating.

"Kalani!" Ani called out, waving Kal over to the table. "You should hear this, too. It's important."

Kal came over and took a seat at the table. "What is it, Tūtū?"

"I had an important dream last night."

"About what?" Kal asked.

Ani reached out and placed her palm on Lana's stomach the way everyone else had been touching Paige. "About your son."

Lana stiffened in her seat, looking to Kal in surprise. Their son? "But I'm not pregnant."

Ani laughed and shook her head. "You may not realize it yet, but you are, you are. Your son will be tall and strong, like a Hawaiian god forged from the great fires of Mount Kilauea. Keahilani will be the family successor, the one to lead the family when I am gone, and you are gone."

Kal looked just as startled as Lana was. "Are you certain, Tūtū?"

The old woman narrowed her eyes at them in irritation. "Of course I am. I had the same dreams about you and Mano when your mother was carrying you. That's how your names were chosen—our ancestors spoke to me through dreams and showed me who you would be. You were to be chieftain and your brother arose from the sea and swam with the sharks in my dreams. Your son will be Keahilani—from heaven's fire. I have seen it."

Ani got up from her chair and leaned in to give Lana a kiss on the cheek. "*Ho'omaika'i 'ana* to you both."

Lana and Kal sat dumbfounded at the table as Ani congratulated them and wandered away to talk to someone else. They watched her fade into the crowd. Then they turned to each other and looked down at her still-flat belly.

"Could she be right?" Lana asked.

Kal just grinned and leaned in to give her a kiss. His touch sent a thrill through Lana's whole body, making her wish they were alone together in bed instead of surrounded by family at an event they couldn't escape.

"She always is. Keahi is on his way and our beautiful family has begun."

* * * * *

*If you liked this story of a billionaire tamed
by the love of the right woman—and her baby—
pick up these other novels from
Andrea Laurence*

*MORE THAN HE EXPECTED
HIS LOVER'S LITTLE SECRET
THE CEO'S UNEXPECTED CHILD
THE PREGNANCY PROPOSITION*

Available now from Harlequin Desire!

***

And don't miss the next
BILLIONAIRES AND BABIES *story*
ONE BABY, TWO SECRETS
by New York Times *bestselling author*
Barbara Dunlop
Available January 2017!

***

*If you're on Twitter, tell us what you think
of Harlequin Desire! #harlequindesire*

MILLS & BOON®
Hardback – December 2016

ROMANCE

A Di Sione for the Greek's Pleasure	Kate Hewitt
The Prince's Pregnant Mistress	Maisey Yates
The Greek's Christmas Bride	Lynne Graham
The Guardian's Virgin Ward	Caitlin Crews
A Royal Vow of Convenience	Sharon Kendrick
The Desert King's Secret Heir	Annie West
Married for the Sheikh's Duty	Tara Pammi
Surrendering to the Vengeful Italian	Angela Bissell
Winter Wedding for the Prince	Barbara Wallace
Christmas in the Boss's Castle	Scarlet Wilson
Her Festive Doorstep Baby	Kate Hardy
Holiday with the Mystery Italian	Ellie Darkins
White Christmas for the Single Mum	Susanne Hampton
A Royal Baby for Christmas	Scarlet Wilson
Playboy on Her Christmas List	Carol Marinelli
The Army Doc's Baby Bombshell	Sue MacKay
The Doctor's Sleigh Bell Proposal	Susan Carlisle
The Baby Proposal	Andrea Laurence
Maid Under the Mistletoe	Maureen Child

MILLS & BOON®
Large Print – December 2016

ROMANCE

The Di Sione Secret Baby	Maya Blake
Carides's Forgotten Wife	Maisey Yates
The Playboy's Ruthless Pursuit	Miranda Lee
His Mistress for a Week	Melanie Milburne
Crowned for the Prince's Heir	Sharon Kendrick
In the Sheikh's Service	Susan Stephens
Marrying Her Royal Enemy	Jennifer Hayward
An Unlikely Bride for the Billionaire	Michelle Douglas
Falling for the Secret Millionaire	Kate Hardy
The Forbidden Prince	Alison Roberts
The Best Man's Guarded Heart	Katrina Cudmore

HISTORICAL

Sheikh's Mail-Order Bride	Marguerite Kaye
Miss Marianne's Disgrace	Georgie Lee
Her Enemy at the Altar	Virginia Heath
Enslaved by the Desert Trader	Greta Gilbert
Royalist on the Run	Helen Dickson

MEDICAL

The Prince and the Midwife	Robin Gianna
His Pregnant Sleeping Beauty	Lynne Marshall
One Night, Twin Consequences	Annie O'Neil
Twin Surprise for the Single Doc	Susanne Hampton
The Doctor's Forbidden Fling	Karin Baine
The Army Doc's Secret Wife	Charlotte Hawkes

MILLS & BOON®
Hardback – January 2017

ROMANCE

1216 GEN STD HB

MILLS & BOON®
Large Print – January 2017

ROMANCE

To Blackmail a Di Sione	Rachael Thomas
A Ring for Vincenzo's Heir	Jennie Lucas
Demetriou Demands His Child	Kate Hewitt
Trapped by Vialli's Vows	Chantelle Shaw
The Sheikh's Baby Scandal	Carol Marinelli
Defying the Billionaire's Command	Michelle Conder
The Secret Beneath the Veil	Dani Collins
Stepping into the Prince's World	Marion Lennox
Unveiling the Bridesmaid	Jessica Gilmore
The CEO's Surprise Family	Teresa Carpenter
The Billionaire from Her Past	Leah Ashton

HISTORICAL

Stolen Encounters with the Duchess	Julia Justiss
The Cinderella Governess	Georgie Lee
The Reluctant Viscount	Lara Temple
Taming the Tempestuous Tudor	Juliet Landon
Silk, Swords and Surrender	Jeannie Lin

MEDICAL

Taming Hollywood's Ultimate Playboy	Amalie Berlin
Winning Back His Doctor Bride	Tina Beckett
White Wedding for a Southern Belle	Susan Carlisle
Wedding Date with the Army Doc	Lynne Marshall
Capturing the Single Dad's Heart	Kate Hardy
Doctor, Mummy... Wife?	Dianne Drake